Presented to

Hannah McLeish

Arngask

Sunday School

2006

Children's Ministry • KKP00004

children. Her interests include dance, theatre,
music and escaping into the countryside.

*For Sarah Pawlett,
and with thanks to the Hood family*

THE
life shop

Margaret McAllister

LION
CHILDREN'S

Text copyright © 2004 Margaret McAllister

The moral rights of the author
have been asserted

A Lion Children's Book
an imprint of
Lion Hudson plc
Mayfield House, 256 Banbury Road,
Oxford OX2 7DH, England
www.lionhudson.com
ISBN 0 7459 4906 1

First edition 2004
10 9 8 7 6 5 4 3 2 1 0

A catalogue record for this book is available
from the British Library

Typeset in 11/16 Garamond ITC Lt BT
Printed and bound in Great Britain
by Cox & Wyman Ltd, Reading

1

Even to this day I hate to see those colours together, shiny holly green and that golden yellow. It's funny to think that I hardly noticed them on that fat, glossy catalogue I saw at Fern's house. Naturally, it would be at Fern's house. In those days we had a running joke going about her mum, Queen of the Catalogues.

I really like Fern's mum – Mrs Miller, I should say – she's mumsy and kind. The thing is, she's always been a complete sucker for mail-order shopping. It must run in the family, because Fern's a bit like that too, and so's her dad. Her brother Kieron's not, but Kieron's different. He's a one-off. (So's my own brother, but in another way.)

Fern's mum was the Mail-Order Momma of Hutton Park. You'd always find a stack of catalogues on a table, one on the chair where Fern's dad was about to sit down, two propped up in their wrappers by the front door, and the cat eating another one. You could have papered Buckingham Palace with them. I don't think she ever went out and bought anything, except at the supermarket.

I'm not exaggerating. Well, not much. It wasn't just clothes, all the kitchen stuff was mail order, too, and the household things:

'Nice duvet cover, Fern.'

'Mum bought it from a catalogue.'

'I like your new wallpaper.'

'Mum got it on order.'

Kieron's new computer? Furniture? Everything. At Christmas she ordered every single present, the tree, the cake, the pud, and if anyone had come up with a self-stuffing turkey she'd have had that, too.

Fern's dad was into wildlife gardening – frogs and bogs, that sort of stuff. OK, so you can't buy mail-order frogs, but he got some seriously weird stuff for feeding to hedgehogs.

I reckon they ordered Kieron and Fern from the de luxe section. *Kids to go.* One boy, please, a science whizz kid, and absolutely, knock-out, walking-into-lamp-posts gorgeous. (Lots of the girls in my year fancied him, and I sometimes did, but he was more like a big brother.) And one girl, so pretty you'd think nobody would like her for long. But you can't help liking Fern.

You can tell straight away that those two are brother and

sister, they're both dark with that sort of Mediterranean skin and glossy hair, and deep brown eyes. Fern always looks as if she's about to laugh, because she is. She sparkles. We've been friends since we were little, and we used to do our homework together most evenings.

I was staying at Fern's house overnight when Mum was away in Newcastle, taking Charlie – my little brother – to see his specialist for two days of tests and assessments. Fern and I were working together on a project about the Tudors. We didn't have to hand it in for months, but there's a lot you can do about the Tudors (some of it's pretty racy, really), so we wanted to get started on it early. She'd done some drawings and spread them out across her bedroom floor – queens in fantastic gowns with long wide sleeves, and black-and-white wonky houses with little windows. One of those houses had 'The Countess of Essex' written over the door, tubs of purple pansies outside, and a sign pointing to the car park.

'That isn't Tudor,' I said, and then I realized what she was doing. 'Is that your restaurant?'

'It's a Tudor-themed restaurant,' she said proudly, and smoothed the drawings across the carpet. 'I could call it "Queen Bess" or "Lady Jane's", but that's too obvious.'

Fern's dream was to run her own restaurant. She'd talked about it for as long as I could remember. She planned to train as a chef and have a restaurant that would be completely different from anything else anyone

7

had ever done. We must have spent hours planning Fern's restaurant. Sometimes it was going to have an aquatic theme, all blue and green with enormous fish tanks and pools everywhere, or else it was to be like a starry night with everything deep blue and silver; then we went to see *A Midsummer Night's Dream*, and after that she wanted an enchanted forest. We used to plan the menus, decor, uniforms, you name it – we could have opened restaurants from Montreal to Middlesbrough. I wasn't sure about Tudor food, though.

'You're not going to do roast swan, are you?' I said.

'We'd have to offer game,' she said, and added a Tudor sort of squiggle to a corner of the picture. 'And roast boar…' And she was off, with serving wenches and pageboys and minstrels. It all sounded too Olde Englande Merry-My-Lord to be true, but that didn't matter, because none of Fern's ideas lasted for long. She'd be into something else in a month.

Anyway, we discovered that we didn't know a lot about Tudor food, so we went to Kieron's room to ask if we could do a search on his computer.

Er… exactly how much have I told you about Kieron? His room looks like a flight deck of a spaceship. He's always into something new. He was so into computers he could have taken over the world, then he discovered multimedia and it was all digital cameras and studios. He was in the sixth form, and doing dogsbody sort of work for a photographer at weekends, mostly weddings.

He glanced up from his desk, said something like, 'Hi, Lorna, cool, yeah, whatever,' and shuffled over while we checked out loads of websites and found out more than we ever wanted to know about Tudor food. *Don't go there.* You wouldn't believe what they used to do with a dead peacock. The only thing more disgusting than a Tudor kitchen was a Tudor doctor's consulting room. By the time we were through we had some revolting stuff for our project and Fern had decided she didn't want to run a Tudor restaurant any more. She did suggest theming it around a play we were studying, called *Dr Faustus*, but I told her to get real, because *Dr Faustus* is scary and weird. It's about a brilliant man who makes a pact with the devil. With all his education, he should have known better. At the end it's payback time and he's dragged off to hell, so if I saw a restaurant called 'The Faust House', I'd run the other way. Then we remembered what we were supposed to be doing, and we were in Fern's room writing up our notes when Mrs Miller came upstairs, a bit out of breath, and asked me about Charlie.

'He's still about the same, thanks,' I said. 'He's managing a few steps without sticks. And he still takes Peter Rabbit everywhere.' It was important to mention that, because his Peter Rabbit toy was a present from the Millers on his sixth birthday. It still looked surprisingly good, considering Charlie had been hauling it around for six months.

'Poor little Charlie, little love, it's so sad, your mum's wonderful with him,' said Fern's mum. (She doesn't waste time on full stops.) She's one of those cuddly, well-padded mums, and she adores Charlie. 'You too, Lorna, you're a lovely sister, but what a shame he's the way he is.'

'He's OK,' I said. 'He's happy, that's what matters most.' He didn't know there was anything the matter with him, did he? I often wondered what he would have been like if things had been different, but you can't help doing that with a child like Charlie.

'I saw something in my new catalogue that he'd like,' she said, so of course Fern and I caught each other's eyes and got the giggles. I should have known better than to look at her. Fortunately her mum left the room before the spluttering started, and didn't notice it when she came back in. She was too absorbed in the catalogue.

'It's new, this,' she said, 'and it's very good, has your mum got one, 'cause I can order her one.' She licked her finger and flicked through the shiny pages, muttering to herself, 'That's nice,' and, 'That would be useful for the garden,' before she found the right page and turned it towards me.

'Chime bars,' she said, 'nice solid metal ones, they're all different colours, your Charlie's like you, he likes music, doesn't he?'

He did, but what sort of a racket would he whack out of those chime bars? They looked seriously hefty to me.

'They're very nice,' I said politely. 'What's the catalogue?'

She closed it to look at the front and smiled kindly, as if she wanted to make friends with it. 'It's called "The Life Shop",' she said. 'You can get anything and everything from here, absolutely everything, all from the same catalogue, and all reasonably priced, I'm most impressed, they used to just do clothes and household, now they do everything, whatever you could want, and holidays and that.' She handed it to me. I suppose it wasn't a completely new company – come to think of it, people had been wearing its stuff for ages, but I hadn't noticed. And that was the first time I saw that shiny green and yellow cover, the bright brash title and the radiantly smiling picture on the front.

'That's Cassandra Catto,' she said, though of course everybody knew who Cassandra Catto was because in those days she was never off the television. 'Cassandra Catto does adverts for them, I'll get one for your mum, there's sure to be something in there that she wants, sure to be.'

That's how it all started. Looking back, I can't believe that I simply took it without thinking. But at that time, I didn't know.

2

By the time Mum came back the next day, I'd forgotten about the Life Shop. It was only a catalogue, for heaven's sake. Mum had spent most of the morning at the hospital, driven back from Newcastle, dropped Charlie at his school for what was left of the afternoon, talked to his headmistress and then done the shopping. By the time I came in from school she'd flopped. I found her looking as worn out as the old armchair she'd collapsed into. She was more than tired. She was used up and, in a way, defeated. I made a pot of tea and put my mug on the mantelpiece, because I'm in the habit of putting things where Charlie can't knock them over even when he's not there.

'Let's hear all about it,' I said.

Mum sighed, hauled herself up and sipped at her tea. 'They haven't found out much that we didn't already know,' she said. 'They're still not sure exactly what his problem is. Something in the area of cerebral palsy with learning difficulties, but we already knew that, and they still don't know what extent of cerebral palsy.' Then she straightened her shoulders and smiled bravely. 'But Dr Montgomery's developed a programme specially for him.'

Dr Montgomery, the consultant, was really good. He was a kind, quiet man who looked like a nice grandfather, and he was encouraging without giving any false hopes. Mum brightened up as she told me about Charlie's programme, and all the games and exercises we had to do with him. He'd have all sorts of therapists working with him at school, but we could do a lot at home, too. Dr Montgomery was very keen for him to do music, and I could take care of that. There were games, and exercises to do, too, for his walking and co-ordination. We hoped he could learn to read and write, even just a little. He could recognize a few words and write his name, though if you didn't know it was Charlie Young you'd never work it out.

'We have to make the most of his potential,' said Mum, and pushed straggling corkscrews of hair out of her eyes. 'Or rather, *he* does. It's going to mean a lot of hard work all round.'

'Fine,' I said. I was so glad there was something we could do, I couldn't wait to get stuck into Charlie's programme.

'I keep wondering about you, Lorna,' she said. 'It's a struggle now, but when I'm not here…'

Here she goes, I thought. When I'm old, when I can't look after him any more, and there's nobody but you… That's how she always talked if she was getting depressed over Charlie, which didn't happen all that often. Mum's the lean, fit type who looks as if she can cope with anything. Come to think of it, she practically can, but it's harder than it looks.

'You're not on your Zimmer frame yet, Mum,' I said. 'And I don't mind looking after him when you hit the Horlicks and free teeth.' I ducked 'cause I thought she'd throw a cushion at me. 'I'll be there for him, Mum, as long as he needs me. And there's Dad.'

'There isn't, mostly,' said Mum.

'Well, at least he sends money,' I said. 'It's something.'

She didn't reply, and I didn't push it. Dad had scarpered with the babysitter when Charlie was a baby. It wasn't Mum's fault, or mine, either. We kept telling each other that. And what had Charlie ever done to upset him, apart from being born with a disability? But there wasn't time to talk about Dad, because a car was drawing up outside.

'Charlie's taxi!' I said. I'd know that grumbling engine anywhere, and it lifted my heart every time. I ran to the door as the escort helped him out.

'Hi, Charlie!' I called. Suddenly, everyone was smiling!

Charlie does that to people. The thing is, when you first look at him, he doesn't look different. He's blond, bright and beautiful, with the sort of eyelashes that are wasted on a boy, and his smile is just so magical! He broke into that dazzling beam when he saw me and came waddling up the path with his sticks, holding his arms out for a hug. How can a little boy be disabled and perfect at the same time?

I was dying to take his hand but I had to let him manage the doorstep on his own, and he did it, too, with only one hand on the rail before he lurched giggling into my arms. Mum came to the door and glanced up past us. Some of the girls from my year at school were walking past.

'Everyone's wearing those sandals this year,' she said thoughtfully. 'It's way too early for sandals, but they're into them already. Those grey strappy ones. All the girls in Newcastle were wearing them, too.' I was on my knees on the floor, helping Charlie off with his jacket while she leaned over to try to see my feet. 'Do you need new sandals?'

'I like my old ones,' I said. It seemed like a funny question to ask in a spell of wellies weather. It was only March, and I had no intention of getting frostbite around my toes, even if everyone else did. I put Charlie's jacket over my head so he could pull it off, because he thought that was hilarious. I just love Charlie's giggle. You could bottle it to sell, but nobody could afford it, it's priceless. Mum was still asking me about the sandals.

'I'm not bothered, Mum,' I said, though now she mentioned it I had a feeling I'd seen Fern wearing some, but Charlie was waddling to the piano so I sat him on my knee and we played 'The Teddy Bears' Picnic' – that was his favourite at the time. When I say 'we', I mean I held his hands and put his fingers on the keys. We always play the piano like that.

For some reason that I couldn't understand, Mum kept on about sandals. I was right about Fern, she did have a pair of those grey strappy ones. So did most of the girls. Within a few weeks, she had the suede bag to go with them, too. I noticed it when I went to the Millers' house one day after school, to collect Charlie. (His school had a training day and Mum was working, so Mrs Miller was looking after him.) I held Fern's bag while she opened the door, and from somewhere in the house I heard a little tune – no, not exactly a tune, just a sequence of notes. It was a simple six-note pattern, like a jingle. It wasn't quite right – the timing was a bit out – but all the same, I knew I'd heard it somewhere. A very large bottom in stretch jeans loomed at us from the middle of the sitting-room floor. Mrs Miller was on her hands and knees with Charlie.

'Oh, Mum,' said Fern, 'are those Charlie's chime bars? He's supposed to play them, not you.'

'We're having a lovely time, aren't we, Charlie?' she

said, a bit too loudly – there's nothing the matter with his hearing. 'They're the ones out of that Life Shop catalogue, he loves them, don't you sweetheart, show your Lorna what you've learned.' She turned as Charlie stumbled into my arms for a hug.

'That's very kind,' I said over Charlie's shoulder as I cuddled him, but Mrs Miller flapped a hand at me.

'Get away, the Life Shop had a special offer on, you order a copy for a friend and you get a freebie, so I got Charlie's chime bars, your mum's catalogue's on the table there, for you to take home.'

'It's very kind, all the same,' I said.

'No, you're welcome, and I got another freebie for spending more than sixty pounds on one order and I got Fern's bag, do you like it, it goes with the sandals, Charlie, are you going to show your Lorna what you can do?'

She gave him the beater, and he lowered himself carefully onto the floor so he could wallop out a few notes. He laughed up at me, looking very proud of himself.

'Play Lorna your little tune,' said Mrs Miller, and took the beater. It was that same six-note sequence again, but there were only three different notes in it. What was really irritating was that I still couldn't pinpoint where I'd heard it before. Then the door banged, a holdall hit the floor, a voice shouted 'Hi!' to everyone within five miles, and Kieron was home. He didn't come in, just charged up to the flight deck, but soon he was downstairs again.

'Hi, Lorna, I've downloaded some more Tudor stuff,' he said. 'It's on the dining-room table, if you want to come and see it.'

Um… was this a 'you and me alone' moment? Fern was on the floor playing with Charlie, so I went with Kieron to the dining room, where the French windows lead out to the garden. Kieron shut the doors behind us, pushed some computer print-outs and various Tudor stuff at me without even looking, and walked to the window.

'Dad's been out with the weedkiller,' he said.

Romantic, not. Not so much 'down to earth with a bump' as 'never got off the ground in the first place'. He stood with his arms folded, staring out of the French windows.

'What do you think about all this?' he said.

I stood beside him and looked out at the garden. 'It's very neat,' I said.

It was. How short can a lawn be? That grass had been shaved, never mind cut. Every bush was trimmed, all the deadheads of flowers had been snipped off. The far end of the garden always used to be rambling and overgrown, because Mr Miller said it attracted wildlife. Well, tough luck on the wildlife. It just wasn't there any more. It had all been cleared, weeded and turned over. There were neat rows of smug little rose bushes and twee dinky bedding plants. It was all as tidy as an empty house.

'I don't understand it,' said Kieron. 'This is just the sort of garden Dad hates.'

'Maybe he's just trying things out,' I said. 'Experimenting with different ways of doing – um – flowers. Shrubs and stuff.' But I didn't convince me, let alone Kieron. He didn't reply, just looked out of the windows with that brooding expression, so I tried again.

'He's only trying something new,' I said. 'Like Fern always trying a new restaurant, or when I wanted to learn drumming, or...'

'It's not the same at all,' he said. 'Dad's old enough to know what he cares about, and he cares about the environment. He could have won a Green Anorak badge. Then he suddenly ordered all this lot and enough chemicals to start a bomb factory, got stuck in and created the kind of garden he always made rude remarks about.'

'Have you said anything to him?'

'May as well talk to a brick,' he said. He still wasn't looking at me. 'He just says, "Doesn't it look great? Wait till it's all finished, better than all those straggly bushes, and it'll be dead easy to look after." He doesn't seem to see what he's doing. Mum doesn't, either, and neither does Fern, because they're too busy drawing circles round things in their catalogue. I thought *you'd* understand.'

Ouch. 'I do,' I said. 'I do understand, but...'

He turned to me at last with a half-hearted fake of a

19

smile. 'Cool,' he said, and I knew he wished he hadn't bothered telling me.

It was time to take Charlie home. I took Mum's copy of the Life Shop catalogue, too. It was heavy enough to cripple a carthorse and I didn't think Mum would be interested, but when she saw it her eyes lit up and she pounced on it like a chocoholic on a Mars bar. She'd seen one at work and loved it.

Charlie's new programme was enough to take my mind off things. The thing is, a child as contented as Charlie can be dead cushy to look after. He didn't demand fun, or get into mischief. That was easy, but it wasn't good for him. So that evening, Mum, Charlie and I did his games, his exercises and his music, and we let him wham bish-bam-zunk out of those chime bars and he loved it, giggling and bouncing all the way through. By the time he was bathed and in his pyjamas with Peter Rabbit under his arm I don't know if he was exhausted, but I was. Mum made hot chocolate and I just flopped, then she put her feet on the settee and flicked through the catalogue. As far as she was concerned, that was a good night out.

Mum didn't go out much, except occasionally with a few friends from work or to fundraising things for Charlie's school. There'd been a couple of guys who were good friends for a while, but nothing ever came of it.

One night, I'd heard her talking to her friend on the

phone. All right, I shouldn't have been listening, but have you never done it? She was laughing about something, then she said, 'Yeah, tell me. "Good-looking professional male, caring personality, would like to meet exhausted divorcee in late thirties, teenage daughter, disabled son, permanently skint, GSOH." You don't see many adverts like that. If I do, I might go for it.'

She was just being funny and she hadn't meant me to hear it, but I thought about it a lot. She doesn't go on much about money, but I don't like to ask for anything. And you should see the car. No, you shouldn't. If it keeps going a bit longer it'll be old enough to sell to a museum, assuming it can get there and depending what drops off on the way.

We get allowances because of Charlie, but it doesn't take care of everything. We have to be careful about what he eats, and getting him places is expensive. Didn't I tell you he's priceless?

After I'd heard that conversation I said I didn't want any more piano lessons. Well, it was true, wasn't it? I could already play the piano, I knew all I needed to know. Anyway, that evening, after doing Charlie's exercises and putting him to bed, I was too exhausted to bother with the piano, so the next day I had to do some practice after homework. When I came downstairs, Mum was putting the television on. I could hear a chatty voice, and laughter.

'I'm putting it on for the holiday programme,' she said.

'This is Cassandra Catto's chat show, but don't worry, it's nearly finished.'

The screen was full of Cassandra Catto's face. She had that bright, patronizing way of talking, as if she were presenting a show for idiots.

'... from all of us here, goodnight,' she said, or goodbye, or get lost, or whatever her signing-off line was. She was one of those very beautiful women, Italian-looking beautiful. She was always on television and slightly more famous than the *Mona Lisa*, but nobody could say what made her famous in the first place. Then the closing music came up and something struck me, something about the signature tune – then it faded out and it was time for the holiday programme. I'd have to wait a bit longer to play the piano. Mum was half watching television and half flicking through the catalogue.

'Your birthday's coming up at the end of the summer,' she said.

'That's months and months away!' I said. 'We haven't had Easter yet!'

She mentioned that there were some nice jackets in there and I said I didn't want one, though I hadn't even seen them. But after Mum had finished with it, I curled up with the catalogue on my knee. I'd nearly dislocated my shoulder carrying the thing home, I might as well see what was in it.

Catalogues are addictive. No, really, they are! The Life

Shop catalogue was like a shopping mall: you could stay in it all day and have your lunch in there and still not see everything there was – clothes, household stuff, garden things, electrical gizmos. And just when you thought it sold everything except pink kangaroos and the Crown Jewels, there were extra pages at the back: 'Phone this number to ask about our grocery-delivery service, or our book-ordering service... our theatre-booking service... our holiday agency...' By the time I got to financial services and pet insurance I was losing the will to live.

'Aren't you going to bed tonight?' said Mum.

I looked at the clock. I'd spent three hours lost in that catalogue! I hadn't touched the piano, or given a thought to Charlie's exercises.

Whatever was in it, I knew I didn't want any of its stuff for my birthday. Don't ask me why, I just didn't.

I couldn't sleep that night. It was as if my brain had been so pelted with *shop-shop-shop* that it couldn't switch off. And even when I did fall asleep that night, the Cassandra Catto signature tune was in my head, round and round, as if I were trapped in a hamster wheel and couldn't get out.

I had a lot of sleepless nights after that.

3

Mind you, in spite of my doubts about the Life Shop, Fern and I did incredibly well out of it for the next few months. We never bought anything, but Mrs Miller just never stopped. Whenever she ordered something new we caught the old one before she could throw it out, like dogs sitting under the table.

She bought a new microwave though there was nothing wrong with the old one, so Kieron claimed that for when he was ready to go to university. She got new curtains so we got the old ones, which were deep pink and gold. Fern and I reckoned we could make a convincing Tudor costume out of them. (Why make a Tudor costume? Because it's fun, good for a few extra marks, and you never know when you might get invited to a fancy-dress party.) She threw out the old laundry basket, too, so we grabbed it, turned it over, cut a hole in the bottom and used it as a farthingale, which makes the Tudor skirt stick out.

Let me tell you, if you've never seen your best friend wearing a pair of curtains and a laundry basket, you haven't lived. I'd just got the thing fitted around Fern – not easy, she was laughing fit to rupture her ribcage – when she lost her balance, fell over backwards and got the laundry basket jammed up round her ribs. She couldn't get up, and there was no way I could get her on her feet – with all that pink brocade I couldn't even see her feet, but they were nearer the ceiling than the rest of her. I reckoned I needed either Kieron or the fire brigade, so I yelled for Kieron and between the two of us we heaved her the right way up. She was still stuck in the laundry basket and Kieron was about to take his Swiss army knife to it when Fern shrieked – she was wearing some silvery jeans that were another Life Shop craze, and she was terrified he'd cut them. Then her mum came in to see what the noise was about.

'It's our history project, and Fern's stuck in a basket,' I spluttered, and none of us could say anything else after that.

Fern's mum was the only one not laughing. 'When I was at school, projects were about writing up notes, and drawing pictures,' she said.

'But you said we could have this stuff,' said Fern, dusting herself down. I picked up the pictures of her

25

latest restaurant off the floor. She'd landed on them, so they were a bit basketed.

'Well, don't make so much noise about it,' snapped Mrs Miller, as she turned to the door.

'Are you all right, Mum?' asked Fern. She was still struggling with her curtains.

'Why shouldn't I be?' said her mum, and off she went in a cloud of huff.

The giggling stopped. Fern and I stared at each other, then we looked at Kieron.

'Is she really all right?' I said.

'She's not herself,' said Fern. 'She must be worried about something.'

'She's different these days,' said Kieron. 'She's not like our mum.'

'Maybe she's just got a headache or something,' I said, but Kieron wasn't having any.

'Come on, Lorna, if she gets a headache she takes a couple of tablets,' he said. 'It's like Dad and his garden. It's as if their personalities have taken a holiday. She was a bit offhand yesterday, and she's still the same. Even with you, Lorna.'

He had a point there. Parents are usually nicer to other people's kids than they are to their own. And she hadn't asked about Charlie. Kieron was right. She wasn't herself.

I smoothed out Fern's pictures. The restaurant was called 'Silver and Gold' after the colour scheme. She'd worked out her menus, too, and done little sums to cost out the tulle bags of silver and gold almonds on the tables.

'Nice restaurant,' I said, and put my arm round her because I could see her eyes going washy.

'I was going to show those to Mum,' she said, but her voice was all stretched and squeaky and she couldn't say much.

'Maybe your mum's worried,' I said. I never liked to say so, but I wondered how she could afford all that catalogue stuff. 'Maybe it's money? She might owe money to the catalogue people.' My mum hated ever owing money to anyone. She didn't like the idea of being in debt.

'I don't think owing a bit of money would bother her,' said Fern.

'Owing a lot might,' I said.

'Even if it did, she wouldn't take it out on us,' said Kieron. 'Especially on you. It's as if she's lost her…'

'Marbles?' said Fern with a weak giggle. It wasn't all that funny, but I laughed. Kieron didn't.

'Don't be dense, Fern,' he said. 'It's more serious than that. She's lost her… her fun. Her energy. She's like a deflated balloon.'

Even Fern didn't laugh. From downstairs, I heard a familiar phrase of notes from the television. She must have just put it on.

'That's the Cassandra Catto music,' said Fern. She had

a blanked-out look about her, and I thought it was just because her mum had upset her.

'It's not,' said Kieron. 'It's a Life Shop advert.'

Yes, it was. The tune that Mrs Miller had picked out on Charlie's chime bars was a jingle played on the Life Shop adverts. After that, I found I was hearing it everywhere. At the beginning of the year, I'd never even seen the catalogue – but as the days grew longer, everyone was having a Life Shop summer.

The end of summer term came closer and closer, and we crammed in all the work we could on the Tudor project. Did you know, they had laws about who could wear what sort of material and what colour, depending on your rank in society? You started with cloth of gold for royalty and worked your way down. I think they would have dressed the peasants in turnip peelings if there hadn't been some law about buying wool to benefit the sheep farmers.

We learned a bit of *Dr Faustus*, too, but Fern said it was too creepy. And I learned some Elizabethan music and played it with Charlie, putting his fingers on the piano keys. He liked it a lot better than those tinny chime bars. They looked too big and gaudy and you couldn't do much with them. Mostly, you ended up with that same annoying little jingle.

On sunny days, I took him into the garden. I'd play games and chase him to get him moving. We were out there one Saturday afternoon when Mum came out, carrying that wretched catalogue. It was getting as if she couldn't walk without it.

'I thought I'd send for some educational games,' she said, sitting down on the step. 'Something different for Charlie. The Life Shop makes some, and they look very good.'

'But he's got the programme from Dr Montgomery!' I said. What did she want anything else for? She held out the page to me, but I didn't want to see it. I swung Charlie round.

'We could add these to his programme,' she said. 'I can always get them on trial, and we can send them back if we don't like them. If I buy them now I'll get a discount because I've just ordered the tablets.'

'The *what?*' I said. 'What tablets?' This wasn't like Mum. I picked Charlie up because he'd fallen over and couldn't get up again.

'They're just vitamins,' she said with a shrug. 'Specially formulated for children like Charlie.'

'But you can't…'

'Oh, don't be silly, Lorna,' she snapped. 'They've been developed by a doctor, they're perfectly safe.'

'But we shouldn't give him *anything* without asking Dr Montgomery!' I said. Why couldn't she understand that?

Charlie lumbered off after a butterfly and Mum gave me

a look like poison and muttered something about not needing me to tell her how to look after Charlie. I knew she was uneasy about sending for these vitamins, but she was doing it anyway. You don't expect your mum to behave like that, do you? There was no point in arguing, she'd made her mind up. I'd just have to keep the wretched things out of Charlie's way when they arrived.

Anyway, he didn't need tablets. He was doing really well. His walking was getting better and better, and he could move around the garden a lot with sticks and a little without them. Falling down didn't matter, the grass was soft. That afternoon, he was off with a walk like a drunken sailor, pointing and saying ''ose' and ''oopin' and ''oppy' because I'd taught him what all the flowers were.

'And what about you?' said Mum. 'I could order something for you, for school. The Life Shop does an educational pack on Tudor England.'

'There won't be anything in it that Fern and I haven't done already,' I said. 'Thanks, but I don't want it.'

'If you're sure,' she said, and I felt rotten. She wanted to give me a treat, and I was spoiling her fun. But we weren't on the same wavelength any more.

''Aybud!' said Charlie to a ladybird.

'It does adult education, too,' said Mum. Would she never give up? 'And it runs courses. Mrs Miller's going on one and I thought I might, too.'

'What course is she doing?' I asked.

'Something on fashion clothing and retailing,' said Mum.

'Selling T-shirts?' I said. If Mrs Miller could sell them through the Life Shop, she'd be in seventh heaven.

'That's not my sort of thing,' she went on. 'I thought I could do the course on working with disabled children.' She looked up and caught me laughing. 'What's so funny about that?'

'Mum, you could teach it!' I said. Charlie pulled up a dandelion and huffed at it.

'Yes, but if I did a course I'd learn to do it properly,' insisted Mum.

'Then why not write to Dr Montgomery?' I said, as I watched Charlie. 'He'd recommend a course, and tell you how to go about it.'

She went all quiet. Then she murmured, 'Whatever,' and went inside. I'd spoiled her fun again. I suppose she just wanted some happy girly college days with Fern's mum, and now I'd ruined it. What could I do? I put Charlie in his wheelchair with his little wooden boat that Grandpa had made him, and we went to the park, where all the kids were sailing remote-control boats that looked exactly the same. There were girls in silvery jeans and boys in black and silver jackets, and they all looked a bit glazed over, as if they'd been in front of the television too long.

When I did Charlie's exercises with him that night, we tried writing 'L' for 'Lorna', 'lupin' and 'ladybird'. Charlie's effort looked like a tick, but it was something. Oh, and he could do a row of bumps that might be mistaken for 'Mum', so we decided that's what it said.

A tick for Lorna. A tick means 'all right'. But things didn't feel all right. What was so important about some stupid catalogue? Day by day, it seemed to be taking over all our lives.

4

Mum went on dithering about that course – would she, wouldn't she? What I wanted to know was, since when did you buy your adult education along with garden chairs and knickers? If she'd really wanted training she would have asked Dr Montgomery about it, but she didn't want to do a proper course, she wanted to do this one, because by then she was in love with the Life Shop, and it promised it would be easy.

In the end, that problem sorted itself out. Charlie's shoes were falling apart (comes of getting better at walking), he ripped his trousers (comes of not being all *that* good at walking), and then the car needed serious surgery, otherwise we'd all do a lot of walking. So Mum decided she couldn't afford to do the course. That didn't stop the people from the Life Shop ringing us up, though. The first time they tried it their luck was out, because they got me.

'This is Lisa from the Life Shop Education Service,' said the voice at the end. 'Is this Mrs Katherine Young?'

'No, she's out,' I said. (She was bathing Charlie, but near enough.)

'When would be a good time to speak to her?' said Life Shop Lisa. She sounded really pleasant over the phone, like an easy-going Mrs Thingy next door, but I'd already had enough of the Life Shop.

'I've no idea,' I said, and hung up quickly. I didn't tell Mum about that call. I don't know why not. Yes I do. Anyway, Life Shop Lisa got back to Mum later and I heard her saying that she'd got the course details but she didn't want to go ahead with it.

She was on that phone for hours, or that's what it seemed like. There were long silences when she couldn't get a word in if she squeezed it sideways, and when she did say anything it was usually 'but': 'Thank you, but all things considered…'; 'Thank you, but I'd rather not…'; 'Thank you, but it won't be necessary…' Finally, she said, 'Well, maybe at some time in the future…'

That was a mistake. Life Shop Lisa clearly thought that 'some time in the future' meant, 'We've got her hooked and we're not going to let her go without signing up.' Mum looked as if she'd be welded to that phone for the next twenty-four hours, unless either she gave in or I did something.

So I did something. I took an old envelope, a large one,

scrawled 'NO!' with one of Charlie's thick red pens, and held it up. She saw it.

'No, thank you,' she said firmly into the phone. That was more like my mum. Then, 'Thank you, yes, but...'

I popped up from behind the notice. 'No!' I mouthed at her.

'No,' she said again, and she was smiling. 'No, I don't want... yes, you can send me...'

She only had a choice of two words, so why keep getting the wrong one? I shook my head, but she was trying not to look at me and laugh. I grabbed the pen, scrawled the letters on the palms of my hands and waved at her. 'NO!'

She was laughing now. I wished I had Fern there to give her a real fit of giggles, but I was doing pretty well on my own. I flashed my hands, waved the notice in front of her eyes, and mouthed 'NO!'

'Thank you,' she said down the phone, then in a fast tight voice said, 'I must go,' very quickly, as you do when you're about to fold up. She was laughing too much to speak, so I waited till her batteries had run down.

'Took you a long time to say no,' I said.

She told me all about it. They were really nice to her. They'd offered her easy payments and free travel to college. They'd got her to admit that money was a problem, then they'd offered to take over her car insurance or pay for the car's repairs and she could pay them back when she'd finished the course. Or she could put it off, and take it later. She could do it in stages, and if she signed up for that they'd give her the textbook free and a freebie educational toy for Charlie. She could sign up for a different course, a cheaper one, and she'd be less qualified at the end but they'd give her free cinema tickets. She just couldn't get rid of them until I'd told her to stop listening and say no. Then she grinned like a naughty kid.

'You got your hands mixed up,' she said, and showed me what I'd done.

OK, so I'd told her 'ON'. So what, it worked.

She was unspeakably tired that evening. She fell asleep in the armchair and stayed that way so long I was worried. You'd have thought she'd taken on a team of international wrestlers, not the lady from the catalogue.

It might have been just the extra work tiring her out. She was doing a lot of extra hours, and I had a feeling she'd spent more than she meant to on the Life Shop and was worried about paying for it.

My mum might have changed her mind, but there was no stopping Mrs Miller. She couldn't wait to start her course. It meant she wouldn't be around so much to help with Charlie, but it would soon be the summer holidays, and I'd be at home.

The last week of term should have been fun – it usually is – but it went a bit flat that year. Fern and I got ten tons of credits for our Tudor project – work displayed on the walls, excerpts read out in assembly, and all that – but Fern didn't seem to care. Somewhere along the way, it had stopped being important to her, and that rather took the shine off the success for me, too. Funnily enough all the other projects were pretty much the same, with cute soundbites and carefully copied drawings that looked as if they'd been lifted straight from an educational pack called *Tudor England in Thirty Minutes*.

The whole thing just left me feeling so let down, you know? And there was something let down about Fern, too. She didn't laugh much. I missed that giggle. She was getting a glazed-over look, but so were lots of people, including teachers. I hoped it was only an end-of-term thing, but somehow I knew it wasn't.

Just when we thought there was nothing much happening before the holidays, the Head told us in assembly that our MP was due to visit the school. In a week's time! That wasn't a lot of warning for the teachers to get into their headless chicken costumes and flap about squawking, 'Tidy that cloakroom!' 'Clean that classroom!' 'No trainers!' Everybody's best work was pinned on the walls, the link corridor was painted for the first time since 1942, and our Tudor lady costume was put on a tailor's dummy in the hall. (It didn't have a head so everyone called it Anne Boleyn, then just Annie.) The choir had to be wheeled out to sing.

It was a really big do, with TV cameras filming it for the local news. Trevor McLean, MP had just been promoted and was now Trevor McLean, Secretary of State for Commerce and Trade. About twenty of us were chosen to write out questions to ask him. The teachers checked them and threw out the cheeky ones like 'When is your government going to do something intelligent?' and the silly ones like 'Why can't we all move to the moon, and then it won't matter if the earth gets polluted?' I wrote one that I thought was rather cool, about fair trade and developing countries, but mine wasn't chosen.

So the day came, and Trevor McLean, Secretary of State for Whatsit and Thingy, came to school all blond and beaming and well polished around the teeth – you know the sort of thing. Kieron loved it because the TV crew let him play with the cameras, and you've never seen such a squash around the mirrors in the girls' loos. We got as far as the questions. We had to sit around in the hall looking informal and intelligent at the same time (it's cool, try it), though of course it was all set up by the TV crews, with Trevor of the Gleaming Teeth in the middle. I was dying to know which questions had been put forward. We had a captive politician. We could have asked him *anything*, about the government and what they were doing about health, crime, the state of the world, anything. *Anything*. But when the questions came up, they were…

Look, I'm not saying this just because my question had been turned down, right? But those questions were plain daft. 'Where's your favourite place to go on holiday?' 'What subjects did you like at school?' 'What would you do if you won the lottery?' I wouldn't have been surprised if they'd asked him his favourite colour. The teachers had *chosen* those questions. What were they thinking about?

It was all a bit of a lead balloon, anyway. They showed thirty seconds of it on TV, and the next day everybody was talking about other things. Just the usual things, but even that wasn't normal, not that summer.

There are always trends at school, especially in summer. You know, one person starts going round with blue hair, one sandal, a welly and a pink rabbit on their shoulder, and before you know it, everyone's the same. All right, I'm exaggerating again. That summer, everyone was wearing grey sandals like Fern's, with the matching handbags. Then it was tight silvery jeans, and the lads were all wearing the black and silver jackets. When the sun came out, so did the T-shirts, the shades, the sun cream, and the hats, all identical and all from the Life Shop.

Mum had stopped trying to force me into the sandals. With the extra work, she had less time for Charlie and me.

You couldn't have a conversation with anyone. We all used to be able to talk about things from world peace to the World Cup, and make silly jokes about the Head's bald patch. Not any more. In the cloakrooms, the yard, everywhere, the chat never got further than clothes, Mediterranean holidays and Cassandra Catto's show. Everywhere you went, you heard that Life Shop jingle.

Well, it all chugged on to the end of term. Fern and I staggered home on the last day, and I swear to you, we couldn't see where we were going for all the heaps of stuff we had to carry – books, kit that had turned up in the lost-property box and, of course, Headless Annie still attached to her washing basket. Finally I borrowed a skateboard and wheeled her along like a Dalek in drag. Fern sort of laughed, but not the way she used to. In the evening we went out for a Coke and I tried to get her onto her favourite subject.

'What would you do with this,' I asked her, 'if it could be your restaurant?' She said nothing, just sat there with a large Coke and the straw in her mouth, and her deep dark eyes unfocused, as if she were in a trance.

'Silver and gold?' I suggested.

Fern finished soaking up the Coke, detached herself from the straw, flicked her hair and said carelessly, 'I don't want a restaurant. Not my own restaurant. Too much responsibility. I'd rather work in a fast-food place or a motorway service station. Something like that.'

It was as if the sun had gone in.

I can't remember what else we talked about, but we must have talked about something. When I got home I stretched out on my bed and looked at the ceiling. From somewhere in the house I could hear that little tune again, but I heard that everywhere. Suddenly everybody, everywhere I went, was into the Life Shop and Cassandra Catto. That wouldn't have mattered, except that they weren't into anything else, were they? Everyone seemed to be taken in. Even my mum.

Whatever they were getting from that catalogue – holidays, education, or just sandals – they were paying for it with their personalities. Before my eyes, my best friend was disappearing.

Why wasn't it happening to me? I suppose it was just because they didn't offer anything I really wanted.

Kieron was still OK. I needed to talk to him.

5

At Fern's house I found her flicking through the catalogue with her mum and dad watching – yes, there's a surprise – Cassandra Catto on the television. I asked if it was all right to go upstairs (it was a bit awkward, you know, with it being Kieron's room, even though we've known each other for years), but nobody was bothered and I don't know if they even heard me. I tapped at the door, stepped onto the flight deck and wanted to walk straight out again. Oh, no, not Kieron too.

He was in the middle of all the high-tech stuff – stereo, TV, computer, all that – but even on a swivel chair he was slumped like a couch potato with the remote in his hand. Cassandra Catto's face was grinning out of a television and I swear to you, I wanted to kick that screen into fragments.

'I thought you had more sense,' I said sharply. I was

on my way out, but he swivelled round.

'Where are you going?' he said.

'Out,' I said. 'Out, to somewhere there's no television and no Catlitter Cassandra and her Buy-a-Lie Shop, if there's anywhere like that left on earth.'

'Sit down,' he said. He was so bossy I stayed still.

'Please?' I said.

He turned down the volume and moved some books off a stool. *'Please,'* he said, making it very exaggerated as if I'd asked him to get down on his knees. 'Sit down and watch this. I'm serious, Lorna. You need to see this.'

'I didn't come here to watch television.'

'I know you didn't,' he said. 'You came here because you and me are the only people left around here who haven't fallen for this stuff. Now, watch.'

He flipped across the channels. One, as I said, was Cassandra Catto. The next two were showing adverts, one for the Life Shop's sale catalogue and one for a range of baby products, and I don't have to tell you who sold them. The fourth was a gardening programme, and that was full of the stuff Fern and Kieron's dad had been putting in his garden.

'Let's see what's on after the adverts,' I said. 'It can't all be the Life Shop.'

'It must be the news,' he said, and it was, and that really did come as a surprise, because we were looking at our school.

'They're showing that bit about Trevor McLean again,' said Kieron.

'But that was weeks ago,' I said, 'and it was no big deal at the time.'

'Yes, but they're showing it because he's in the headlines, he's just sorted out some new contract or something,' said Kieron, with his eyes on the screen. 'It's for British computer companies selling overseas.'

He flicked over to a sports programme. It was cricket, but all around the ground we could see green and yellow hoardings because the Life Shop was sponsoring it.

'I'm sick to death of it,' I said. 'Why isn't everybody else?'

'Good question.' Kieron stopped channel hopping and tossed the remote to one side. 'It's sinister. It's into everything, and nobody argues, nobody thinks it's strange. Except us. They all go along with it as if they're hypnotized.'

Exactly. It was no good pretending that this was just some big successful mail-order firm. We both knew there was more to it than that.

'Before we know it, it'll be running all our lives,' he said. 'Somebody has to do something.'

'Like what?' I said.

Kieron's face brightened with such a dazzling smile that suddenly, everything looked a lot better.

'Like get right inside the organization,' he said. He grinned up at me, and his eyes were alight. 'Infiltrate it.

See what it's like from the inside. Look what I've found!' Still grinning, he swivelled to face the computer, tapped a bit and called up the Life Shop website. *'Click on opportunities,'* it said, then, *'Click on training.'*

'I looked this up last week,' he announced. 'I found out about working there, and asked them to give me a placement.'

I opened and shut my mouth twice before anything came out.

'You've done *what?*' I croaked.

'Yeah, and they accepted me!' he said. Bless him. The enthusiasm had spread all over his face. 'I start a week on Monday. They're based in Pellmarket, so it's not too far. It'll be good, I'll get to work in real studios and all that. I'll be making promotional DVDs. Working with their public relations and media people, all that stuff.'

'But you're going back to school in September!' I said.

'It's only a summer job,' he said. 'Except that they regard it as a four-week trial. After that, I can leave or they can sack me.'

'What, you mean, "return within twenty-eight days if not completely delighted"?' I said. He looked puzzled, so I explained. 'It's the sort of thing they put on their guarantee.'

'Is it? Well, I don't mind. I get four weeks of working with cameras, spying on the Life Shop and getting paid for it. I can handle that.'

I wasn't sure he could. 'But you'll go back and finish your A levels, won't you?' I said, and he laughed.

'Sure I will. Lighten up. Want to play some computer games? It's OK, I haven't got any of theirs.'

I might have done, but I wanted to do some music with Charlie before he went to bed. I found him playing with those chime bars – I was sick to death of them by then – so I distracted his attention, hid them and sat him on my lap at the piano. I played little phrases of things and got Charlie plinking 'The Teddy Bears' Picnic' and 'Twinkle, Twinkle, Little Star', but I was running on automatic. My mind was on Kieron. He thought he was James Bond or something, but I was worrying about what he was walking into, or rather, bounding into like an enthusiastic puppy.

The Life Shop was like a drug, but you didn't realize you were taking it. Normal, sensible people just had to pick up the catalogue and place an order, and before you knew it they were hooked. Kieron was going to walk right into that place, but I wasn't convinced the same Kieron would walk out again.

Te tum, tum, te tiddley tum went our fingers on the keys. I played a scale and Charlie thought it was hilarious, but I was thinking about Kieron. You know how you daydream about doing something heroic? I was imagining myself sneaking into the Life Shop to rescue Kieron. Then I thought, why wait for Kieron to need rescuing?

When I look back on it, I know I was just a bit jealous

46

of Kieron. If there was going to be a hero in all this, I wanted it to be me. If Kieron was going undercover, why couldn't I? I didn't know how to go about it, but I'd work something out.

'Music,' said Charlie, and bounced on my lap, so while I was thinking I played a few bars of things he liked – film music, television themes and all that. He started singing and usually he was pretty tuneless, but this time I could hear a phrase.

He was singing *that* phrase. I'd always encouraged him to sing anything, even if he did it badly, but hearing him sing the Life Shop's jingle made my flesh creep.

'That's the wrong music, Charlie,' I said.

'No!' said Charlie, and wriggled round with a beaming smile. I listened to what I was playing, and then snatched my fingers off the keys as if they were stinging.

I'd been playing the theme for the Cassandra Catto show. I hadn't even realized I was doing it. I was just working my way through television stuff, and I ended up playing that, of all things.

I did it again, cautiously, as if it might bite me, but this time I played slowly and listened carefully, playing different themes with the right hand and improvising with the left. There, in Cassandra Catto's theme music, was the Life Shop's jingle. The notes were woven in so subtly that nobody would notice them under the main theme. That's why Fern thought she was hearing the Cassandra Catto theme when it wasn't, it was a Life Shop advert. Whenever you watched that show you heard that jingle, time after time after time.

I closed the piano and read Charlie a Thomas the Tank Engine story. Those stories were written long before there was any Life Shop, or Cassandra Catto, or any of that, and the world must have been safer. Then it was his bedtime, and when he was tucked up I went back downstairs, sat on the floor and played with the chime bars. The range was so limited that whatever you did with them, sooner or later, you'd play that jingle. It blared from the Life Shop's adverts, it crept in with the Cassandra Catto theme, haunting us like a grey ghost, getting inside us like a virus.

Gaining power by getting people into their debt was bad enough, but the music was creeping into hearts and minds. I found I'd turned cold. We were all being brainwashed by that tune, and Cassandra Catto's chat show and her smiling face on the catalogue.

We were all getting so we couldn't live without the Life Shop. We didn't want to. Cassandra Catto and whoever else was behind it had the whole country at their feet. With its cheap-and-cheerful fashions, its holidays, its education, its loan plans, its easy payments, twenty-eight-day returns and credit schemes, and its happy-happy phone lines, it was taking over the country.

6

Mum was out very early in the morning, so it was afternoon before I could tell her about Kieron. I was peeling a banana for Charlie.

'He's going to work for the Life Shop,' I said. 'In Pellmarket.'

'That's nice,' she said airily as she filled the kettle. 'I'm thinking of working for them myself.'

I put the banana down before I could drop it on the floor. 'Since when?' I demanded.

She could tell I was shocked. 'I don't mean moving to Pellmarket,' she said, and laughed. 'I'd be a local agent, working from home. A lot easier than going into an office every day.'

'You'd miss your friends,' I said, but I didn't make a fuss, because she'd only stand up for the Life Shop. As she rooted about in the cupboard for a new jar of coffee I was crossing my fingers, but she didn't find the vitamin tablets that I'd squashed out of the way in a corner.

She'd said she wasn't going to use the vitamin tablets, or whatever they were, but the idea of those people even trying to give Charlie medication made my toes curl. She hadn't actually given them to Charlie, but time and again I'd find her turning the bottle round and round in her hands, reading the little leaflet that came with it.

I'd have to drop them in the bin when she wasn't around, and be ready with a good explanation if she asked where they were. I'd think of something. I grabbed them when she was out of the way, and had one foot on the pedal bin when I remembered I had a brain.

If the Life Shop offered these tablets to Charlie, it must be doing the same with hundreds of children, kids far worse than Charlie, kids whose parents were desperate enough to try anything. Binning them wasn't enough.

I wrote a letter to Dr Montgomery and recycled a Jiffy bag. First thing in the morning, the tablets were in the post. Charlie's consultant should know about this.

Why hadn't Mum thought of that? When I thought of her turning that bottle of tablets round and round I knew she could end up like everybody else, doing whatever the Life Shop told her to do. When you were little, were you ever lost? It was like that. Losing Mum and not knowing if she'd ever come back.

Posting the tablets first class cost more than I'd

expected, and money was a problem. There wasn't much prospect of summer work, so I didn't have much chance of earning anything. Then, soon after Kieron went to work in Pellmarket, Mr Harris rang up.

Lovely old Mr Harris, my piano teacher – my ex-piano teacher, I should say. He'd been asked to play at a wedding but he had to go away, and he'd suggested that I could do it. I wasn't sure, but he took me to the church and showed me how to use the pedals, and I had plenty of time to practise.

Fortunately the bride and groom had chosen pieces I already knew, but not the usual wedding ones. Usually, Mr Harris said, it's WIMO (Wagner In, Mendelssohn Out), and for hymns they go for 'The Lord's My Shepherd' and 'Morning Has Broken', unless it's in the afternoon. (The Life Shop did all that on a CD called *Confetti*.) Anyway, it was a lovely wedding and they paid me in cash, and that made my plan possible. Kieron wasn't the only one going to the Life Shop now.

He'd promised to keep in touch. So far I'd had a text message, saying, *'ARRIVED OK, SPEAK 2U SOON.'* Then there was another one saying how fantastic his flat was and how well everyone there was looking after him. After that I didn't hear anything for a week, so I phoned him.

'It's cool,' he said. 'I'm finding out a lot. I'm going to have to sort a few things out…' Then he somehow changed the subject, and after that he had to ring off.

He never phoned or texted me after that. I tried to call him, but I wasn't getting through. Goodness only knew what was happening. I had to take action.

I rang the Life Shop and, you know, I decided I was wrong about it wanting to take over the world. You could start a counter-revolution in the time it took its staff to answer the phone. If you wish to place an order, press 1; if you wish to order a catalogue, press 2; if you wish to follow up a previous order, press 3; if you wish to talk to an adviser about holidays/financial services/educational opportunities/how to be abducted by aliens, press the number you first thought of, multiply by three and the answer's a lemon. Finally, I got to speak to a real person.

I told him my mum was a customer because I thought it would help, and before I could take a breath he was asking me my age. Fourteen, I said, but it didn't put him off.

'You can order through your mum's account if we have signed permission and a reference,' he said, and rattled off terms and conditions like a well-trained budgie while I tried to interrupt and tell him I didn't want any, thank you, but he wouldn't shut up. Waiting for him to finish, I wondered how many fourteen-year-olds had run up squintillions of debts forging their mothers' signatures.

Finally, he said, 'I can send you details of our next sale…'

'I don't want them, thank you.'

'May I just have a few details about you?'

'No.' I felt I was being really rude to him, but I knew I mustn't get drawn in. It would be so easy, so easy, just to say one tiny little 'yes' to an innocent question, and before I knew it I'd be a vacant-eyed, grey-sandalled clone.

I was holding the phone so tightly my knuckles were white. *Don't agree to anything, don't accept anything.* It was like resisting a magnet. He paused for a moment – I hoped I'd exhausted him – then he said, 'Do you require any other services?'

Services! I nearly asked him if he did weddings and funerals and did he need an organist, but I said, 'Yes, please. I edit our school magazine and I'd really, really like to do an article about the Life Shop. Everyone at school loves your stuff, it's really popular.'

After that I was put through to three different people and got an earful of Vivaldi, but finally I was answered by a man in PR. His name was Simon. How did I know it would be? He sounded like a Simon, a blond one. Within minutes, everything was sorted and he'd fixed me up with a visit to the Life Shop. He even said they'd pay my fare and send the tickets, which was cool, because I'd counted on my music money for that. Charlie was pulling at my sleeve for attention.

'Thank you very much, Simon,' I said.

'Call it an early birthday present,' said Simon with a smile in his voice, and before I could ask how he knew about my birthday he said, 'So I'll see you on the fourteenth of August, at one o'clock. Come and have lunch. Ask for me by name. I'll be there. I'm looking forward to it.'

'So am I,' I lied as I put the phone down. He must have had my details on Mum's file. Then Charlie hit me with Peter Rabbit. He'd never done that before.

My tickets arrived, and so did a letter from Dr Montgomery's secretary, thanking me for sending the tablets and promising to have them analysed. Fortunately I always got to the post first, so Mum didn't notice. But she didn't notice anything much any more. When she wasn't hypnotizing herself with the newest catalogue, she was at work, fitting in all the hours she could. Then it was, 'Lorna, will you be a love and look after Charlie? Only I'm doing a bit of waitressing, just two evenings a week, to help out.'

I didn't mind the babysitting, but that wasn't the point. 'Mum, what's the matter?' I asked. 'Is it money?'

'Don't be cheeky!' she snapped.

I can't tell you how much that hurt. Mum had never, ever been like that with me before. We'd got by without Dad and looked after Charlie, the two of us, and we could have taken on the world. Now she was changing before my eyes, and there was only me to take on the Life Shop.

She hadn't told me, but I knew. She was doing all this extra work because she owed money to the Life Shop.

They wouldn't mind – they'd encourage her to take out more, so she'd have to pay more interest – but Mum hated being in debt. That's why she was snappy. She must have realized I was hurt because after that she was really nice and tried to be interested in what I was doing. She started suggesting pretty things from the Life Shop that I might like for my birthday.

'That's not what I want, Mum,' I said. 'Can't we do something together instead? Go to a concert, or visit somewhere, or something?'

She pursed her lips with that 'faraway thoughtful' look, and my stomach knotted up. I knew, I just *knew* that she was going to get that catalogue out again and tell me that the Life Shop did day trips and discounted visits or tours of Cassandra Catto's television studios. I couldn't stand it. I walked away and played the piano – I had to rub my eyes before I could even see the stupid keys – and played and played and played, and Mum didn't notice a thing.

After I'd played the anger out of my system I did Charlie's exercises with him and got him to practise his writing patterns – he could do something like 'L' now, and I hoped he was trying to write 'Lorna', but he'd never write anything much. Even his own name still looked like a squashed spider. He soon got tired of it, so I took him to feed the ducks. When we got back, Mum was rushing round getting herself together because she was late getting ready for work. I knew why. The catalogue was open on the table.

Every day I rang Kieron to see how he was doing and tell him I was on my way, but his mobile was always switched off, and he didn't seem to be checking messages. Fern still didn't seem to know anything about him and wasn't bothered, and even their mum only said, 'Oh, he seems to be doing fine,' which could have meant anything.

I didn't go to Fern's much any more. It had stopped being my second home. Fern had moved into a different world, and I hadn't. So I went on, looking after Charlie, knocking welly out of the piano, and counting the days until I could go to Pellmarket.

I'd told Mum that I was going for an up-town day on that Thursday, and I'd be late back, and she was fine about it. The day before I thought I'd better remind her, because she'd reached the in-one-ear-and-out-the-other stage. She had the morning off, and was pulling some washing out of the machine. I watched socks and T-shirts tumbling into the basket.

'Mum,' I said, 'don't forget I'm going up town tomorrow.'

'Fine,' she said to the washing, then looked up with a handful of pink knickers (hers). 'You're doing what?'

'I'm going to town tomorrow,' I repeated. 'You said it was OK. I'll get something to eat in town, so don't keep anything for me, and I'll be late back.'

'Oh, Lorna, love,' she said. The knickers dropped

damply into the basket and she pushed her hair out of her eyes. 'I'm so sorry. I forgot. I said I'd work tomorrow.'

'But Mum, you said…'

'I know,' she said. 'Lorna, love, I hate to ask you, but you couldn't make it a different day, could you? I said I'd go into work, and I've got nobody else to look after Charlie.'

'I can't change it, Mum,' I said, and hoped she wouldn't ask why.

'I'll see what I can do,' she said, then she made phone calls to a lot of people who would gladly look after Charlie, but that was the one day they couldn't do it, and they were so very sorry. All her friends seemed to be doing extra hours, as well. In the end, I said I could take him with me.

'But that would spoil your town day,' she said. 'You can't take him into all those shops.'

'It's cool,' I said. It wasn't. Taking Charlie to the Life Shop felt like Mary taking her little lamb to the slaughterhouse. But I'd look after him. With any luck, he might meet Cassandra Catfood and thump her with Peter Rabbit. The way he'd been going on lately, he was capable of it.

7

I was up very early doing Charlie's music exercises with him, because that always put him in a good mood. Mum helped put together the half a ton of heavy engineering we need to get him anywhere. It was a walk to the bus, bus to the station, and a train journey, so I needed his chair and the sticks, too. Mum had given me some money for a day out – I think she felt guilty – so I didn't have to worry about Charlie's fare and I bought him sweets for the journey, too.

Didn't need them, though, did I? So much happened that day, I have to remind myself about Charlie and the station. He'd hardly ever been there before, and he was really into Thomas the Tank Engine and all the other train books. From the moment I wheeled him onto that platform he was sitting up straight in his wheelchair with those bright-blue eyes gazing and gazing at the trains. All the running about, the tannoy announcements and porters with trolleys, all of that went past him and he never noticed. It was the trains, long gleaming green ones and little rattling maroon ones, that had him bolt upright and staring.

That was Charlie. All he had to do was *watch*. He didn't have to *own* things, he didn't grab the way other children do. He pointed and said, 'Ooh!', and we could have stayed there all day, with Charlie content to watch the 10.10 to King's Cross or the half past to Dog's Breakfast or whatever. I hadn't attempted to explain what we were doing, so until our train arrived, he didn't even know he was going anywhere.

'Come on, then,' I said, when the train came into view. As I took him out of the wheelchair he was leaning past me and round me, still trying to see the platform. I hung on to him with one hand and folded the chair with the other. 'Keep hold of my hand. This is our train.'

'Train,' he said loudly, and beamed up at me.

'Our train,' I said again. 'We're going on the train, Charlie!'

'Our train,' he repeated happily, but he still didn't understand.

'Hold tight to Peter Rabbit,' I said, but as I steered us into the cluster of people pressing forward for the door, Charlie stopped. Just stood stone still at the door. I felt his resistance against my hand and pulled, but he'd planted himself on that spot and he wasn't moving.

Great, I thought. What a time to be difficult. I couldn't pick him up without putting everything else down.

'We're going on the train, Charlie,' I said brightly. Then I realized why he was standing still, and it was so obvious. He simply couldn't believe it. He'd been in the car loads of times, but never on a train. I don't know why, but it had never occurred to either of us to take him for a train ride, just for the sake of it. As people wriggled past us, Charlie simply stood with his eyes shining. I honestly think he'd forgotten how to move. There was a porter there in a maroon station uniform, and he was watching us with a big grin on his face.

'Are you going on that train or aren't you, son?' he said. 'Give us your hand, then!'

He was dead nice. He took the chair and held Charlie's hand and helped him manage his first big step on to the train. Then, as the porter pushed the chair between the seats for us, Charlie turned, gazed up as if he'd seen an angel, and said, *'I going on train!'*

'You are, aren't you, son!' said the porter, but now I was the one who stood still, open-mouthed and paralysed. I reminded myself to breathe. Charlie turned his smile to a woman who was already smiling at him and said it again. 'I going on *train!*' Then he beamed up at me and said it to me, *"Orna, I going on train,'* and my eyes filled up and I had to sit down, and Charlie said it to every single person in that carriage, 'I going on *train*, I going on *train*...'

It was his first whole sentence.

'Yes, Charlie,' I said, and hugged him very tightly. 'Isn't it wonderful? You're going on a train!' And Mum wasn't there to hear him.

Everyone on that train fell in love with him. I'd brought his drawing things and stuff, but all he wanted was to stare out of the window at the towns and countryside, pointing things out – cows, sheep, bridges. Whatever happens today, I thought, whatever comes of this, it will have been worth going, if only for this. As we drew nearer to Pellmarket, I heard two women in the carriage talking.

'The Life Shop's somewhere round here, isn't it?' said one. 'I like their stuff.'

'I booked my holiday with them,' said the other.

'I've booked just about everything with them,' said the first, and they giggled like naughty kids. 'My sister's getting her mortgage through them. They're very good about...' Then she lowered her voice, and I heard a few whispers about payments and credit, and before long she had the catalogue on the table and was pointing things out from the back pages. Then there was a tinny tannoy voice telling us that we were approaching Pellmarket Station.

'Time to get off now, Charlie,' I said. He wasn't taking much notice while I got all our stuff together. 'Time to go.'

'I going on train,' he said. Sweet!

'The train stops here,' I said. 'Time to get off the train.'

'I on the train!' said Charlie. With determination he squirmed back in his seat, found the armrest, and hung on tight. 'I on the train!'

I reached for his hand but he glared like daggers and pressed even further away from me. 'I on the train!' His voice was high, tight and tearful, his lips were wobbly and his eyes were filling up. Suddenly everyone was politely ignoring us, but I felt red and hot all the same.

'We're going somewhere very nice,' I coaxed him. I had to say that, I was desperate. 'We'll see if we can get something good to eat.' It wasn't getting me anywhere. I was holding his bag and mine as I reached for him, but the wheelchair was still in the luggage space. That was heavy, and so was Charlie. How did Mum manage at times like this? I wished I knew, because I hadn't a clue what I'd do if he got stroppy, and stroppy was definitely forecast as the voice came over the tannoy again.

'We're now approaching Pellmarket, the home of the Life Shop,' it said. On the tannoy! Weren't things bad enough without that?

'Please make sure you have your bags and all your possessions with you.'

And your little brother in a tantrum, I thought. 'Thank you for travelling with us today.'

Then they played it over the tannoy, that Life Shop

theme! Wasn't there anywhere you could escape from it?

Charlie's face changed. The temper and tearfulness melted away. He was placid. The two women sang the little jingle and laughed. And Charlie took the hand I was holding out, tucked Peter Rabbit under his arm, and came with me without a murmur.

With a bit of help I got the wheelchair off the train and Charlie into it. He still didn't squeak until I wheeled him away, and he twisted round to look up at me with those blue, beautiful eyes.

'Train,' he said plaintively.

I turned him round so he could see it. 'Bye-bye train,' I said, and waved to it, because he understood about waving goodbye. Charlie waved, too, but I could see his bottom lip pushing out. His face reddened. He was gathering himself up for a scene.

I didn't like it, but there was only one thing to do. I leaned down over the chair, and, softly, I sang that little tune in his ear.

It left him as calm and satisfied as if he'd been doped. That was so scary, I almost wished he'd scream and cry instead.

I've heard of drug-addicted mothers who rub a little heroin on their babies' gums to keep them quiet. In the old days, they used laudanum. I sang that tune into Charlie's ear, and I hated myself for it, oh, I was so angry with myself as I swung the chair round and pushed it out of the station through a blaze of green and gold hoardings. The colours of the Life Shop were everywhere, on the awnings of coffee stalls, on posters, on banners and streamers, even in the hanging baskets of flowers. Every single station announcement began and ended with that tune. All around us, happily coming and going on Pellmarket station, I saw people with vacantly smiling faces like Fern's face, like Mrs Miller's, like the way I knew Mum's face would become. Soon everyone's face would be the same if someone didn't stop the Life Shop.

8

Simon, as in Simon in PR, 'ask for me by name', had sent me directions, and soon I was wheeling the chair past long streets of warehouses and office blocks, looking for the Life Shop. I reckoned it would be easy to find, festooned in green and gold with pictures of Cassandra Catto gleaming from every window, but I nearly walked past it. Just a big, plain, rows-of-windows building like the others, with 'The Life Shop' in simple gold lettering over the door, as if it didn't want to draw attention to itself. That wasn't like the Life Shop at all.

The doors glided open for us and the reception area was typical Life Shop.

It was all soft carpets, comfortable chairs around little tables, and everything as sparkling and polished as a showroom. The receptionists looked as if they really enjoyed their work – they smiled, laughed and sang or whistled little snatches of songs that always included the same sequence of notes. But when you looked into their eyes, they were as glazed as porcelain dolls.

It's good for places to be clean, but this was too clean, as if every trace of real life had to be polished away. There I was, hot and bothered, rumpled from the train and the long walk, with all the bags and baggage and a child sprawling in a wheelchair, and I felt like I was something the cat dragged in. Probably looked like it, too. I thought a glassy-eyed cleaner would bring a giant mop and swish us away. The air felt artificial, as if it had been sterilized.

I looked for someone to help me – and there he was, just rising out of a mauve armchair! I was pleased with myself for guessing him so well, but I knew a Life Shop Simon when I saw one. Bleached hair, designer shirt, designer jeans, designer smile, and I suspected he borrowed his teeth from Trevor McLean. He held out his hand.

'Hi! You must be Lorna. I'm Simon.' He squatted down in front of Charlie. 'And who's this?'

'He's my little brother,' I said. 'His name's Charlie. Sorry, but my mum had to work, so…'

'No problem,' he said. He beamed at Charlie, and Charlie beamed back. 'I see you've brought Peter Rabbit with you.'

Charlie pulled out Peter Rabbit from under his arm, held him out by one ear, then tucked him back again.

Simon didn't ask why Charlie was in the chair and I decided not to say anything in case Simon started talking about pills or therapy or something. Besides, I like people to see what's right with Charlie, not what's wrong with him.

'No problem,' said Simon again. 'I'll take you to our crèche, he'll just love it. Would you like to play in the ball pool, Charlie?'

What, so he could come out brainwashed? Fortunately, the words 'ball pool' hadn't registered with Charlie.

'He's shy,' I said. 'He'd rather stay with me.'

'And maybe he's hungry,' said Simon. 'Let's go and have lunch.'

There was a squeaky-clean self-service restaurant with wishy-washy coloured pictures on the walls, and Simon found us a table by a plate glass window, you know, the kind that goes all the way to the floor. It looked down over a pond full of lilies and goldfish, and behind it was a cliff (I'm not sure what that was made of) and a twee little waterfall that gushed down into the pond. Wooden benches were all round it, and the sun was shining, so people were sitting outside with their sandwiches. Music played softly in the background, the kind that goes through your head without stopping. And there was a door leading into that cliff – it sounds like a hobbit hole, but remember, this was the Life Shop. Just a plain door, one that might lead to a storeroom or something.

Simon was still charming and polite while we ate pasta and something tomato and herby. He asked about the journey, and school, and finally I said, 'Can I do my interview now, please?'

He grinned. 'Aren't you already interviewing me?'

You may look like a singer in a boy band, I thought, but you're a patronizing creep all the same. I took out my notebook and pen to show I meant business, while Charlie sat quietly eating pasta shells with his fingers. He looked up and pointed at something.

'Tevision,' he said, which wasn't surprising. The walls were plastered with pictures of celebrities wearing the Life Shop's clothes.

'They're people you've seen on television, yes, love,' I said, then turned to look Simon in the eyes. This was it. Go for the kill.

'A year ago, Simon, I hadn't heard of the Life Shop. Nobody had. And now it's huge, everybody's wearing the clothes and buying the homeware, even ordering holidays and education. How did it get so big so quickly?'

'It's simple,' he said. He leaned back in his chair and crossed his legs. 'We give customers exactly what they want.'

Something odd struck me about that statement. As I wrote it down, I saw what it was.

'You don't *give* it,' I said. 'You sell it.'

Simon laughed. Plainly, that was so obvious that only

a moron would have pointed it out.

'Think of us as a lifestyle supermarket,' he said, smiling. 'But because it's mail order, you don't have to move from your own home. No car parks, no queues, no trolleys, no problems. And no time, because that's the thing everyone's short of. The thing is, Laura…'

'Lorna,' I said.

'I beg your pardon, Lorna, we all spend so much of our time running about organizing our lives, juggling work and family, and there's so much to fit in – shopping to do, insurance to pay, holidays to book – with the Life Shop you can do it all in one go. Fill in a form, pick up a phone, or tap a keyboard. You can buy the whole family's clothes for a season, change your furniture, buy carpets, bedding, kitchen things, do all your Christmas shopping, plan a holiday, take a course and get a qualification, all in the same place. We're looking at a new range just now – this is the newest thing, we're all really excited about it. We're launching *Celebrate!* Parties, festivities. You've got a birthday coming up, yes?'

They must have known my blood group, shoe size, and the colour of my bedroom wallpaper, too, after all those questionnaires Mum had done. It dawned on me that they knew all about Charlie, too – they'd sent him those pills – and that was why Simon hadn't asked about Charlie. He'd been checking the files, and he knew.

'So, have you any plans for your birthday?' he asked.

'We're doing party packs. The basic deal is a present, a cake, presents for your friends, party poppers, a selection of drinks, finger foods and a DVD. The next level up includes vouchers for an afternoon at a leisure centre of your choice and the de luxe version includes all the rest plus crackers, buffet and disco, with optional gorillagram.'

'Gets expensive, surely?' I said.

'Ah, but the Life Shop's offers are brilliant value for money,' he said. (I could imagine him practising his lines in the mirror every night.) 'People out there work hard for their money, and we make sure they get as much as they can for it. For example, the beginning of the new term is coming up. Think about what your mum needs to buy. School uniform.'

'I've got one,' I said, but he wasn't listening.

'Kit, trainers, pens, pencils, rulers, stationery, sticky-back plastic, all that. We can do the whole package at a discount, and throw in a voucher towards educational extras. You, Lorna, might like music lessons, for example.'

'One voucher wouldn't go far,' I said firmly. I reckoned I knew more than he did about the cost of music lessons.

'Oh, I don't know,' he said, and leaned forward with his elbows on the table. 'We have people like you in mind.'

Suddenly he was truly thoughtful and sympathetic. It took me by surprise.

'We put together packages especially for people like you,' he said. 'A really good deal on music lessons, buying or hiring instruments, books, exam fees…'

I forgot to take notes. Simon wasn't patronizing and smarmy any more. He was talking honestly to me about music. We were on a wavelength.

'It's tailor-made, Lorna,' he said gently. There was a little dish of grapes on the table. 'Is it all right for Charlie to eat these? I made sure to get seedless ones.'

I nodded, and he put some on Charlie's plate. He was lovely with Charlie.

'Whatever you think, Lorna,' he said, 'we're not trying to give you what *we* want you to have. We're not hard sell. We know that all our customers are individuals. We're here to provide what *you* want most, without hassle, at a price you can afford.'

Was it too hot in there? Was it the music? My brain had gone a bit fuzzy, and it was hard to think clearly. I looked down at the pond, and that funny little waterfall was so peaceful that it calmed me down. I liked that. I tried to concentrate, telling myself that there had to be a catch in what he'd just said. Struggling against the light-headed feeling, I found it.

'Price I can afford?' I said. 'How do you know what anyone can afford? Do you even have details of your customers' incomes? Their bank accounts?' He started to answer, but I had to cut in before I lost the thread. 'If you sell everything at a price your customers can afford, why are so many of them in debt to you?'

'In debt?' he said. 'I think you're mistaken.'

'I know people who are in debt to you,' I said.

'We don't have debt,' he said gently, and sat back comfortably again. 'Customers sometimes need their purchases urgently, before they can pay for them in full. We don't mind waiting.'

'That's debt,' I insisted. 'If you deliver an order and it hasn't been paid for, they owe you money. That's debt.'

'Debt is the wrong word,' he said. 'We do credit arrangements. Our customers pay on an arranged basis.'

There was something he wasn't mentioning, like a missing clue from a puzzle. The word for it was hiding in my head. The word for paying extra... oh, yes.

'But they pay...' What was the matter with me? It felt as if the word was chained to an anchor, and I had to drag it out of the sludge. 'They pay *interest*.'

Simon looked over the rim of his coffee cup. 'I beg your pardon?' he said lightly.

It had been hard enough saying it the first time. 'Interest,' I said.

There was a silence, but it didn't matter. Saying that word had taken the strength out of me. I sat back, so tired, watching the waterfall. That lovely waterfall, sparkling in the sun, and its soft blue pond where the fish glided, and the music. Simon's voice purred across the table.

'You were talking about your interests,' he said. 'Will you tell me more?'

Were we? It seemed like a good idea.

'It's the piano, isn't it?' he said. 'I think you've done Grade Seven, haven't you?'

If I try to remember it's all very vague, but I know how kindly and thoughtfully he listened to me while I watched the waterfall and the music washed through me and cradled me, and I told him all about Mr Harris, and playing for weddings, and my piano at home. I knew it was impossible to have lessons, but in all that peacefulness, with Simon being so kind, anything at all seemed possible

'Tevision! 'Orna! Tevision!' said Charlie.

'Yes, love,' I said. I wasn't interested, but he pulled hard at my arm and waved Peter Rabbit at me.

'Tevision!' he repeated. He was shaking my arm by now and pointing at the pool. Reluctantly, I looked.

Cassandra Catto! She was walking round the pool towards the door in the artificial cliff. She looked gorgeous in grey and silver with all that gleaming hair, and she walked like a dancer.

'That's Cassandra Catto!' I said. I gave myself a shake because I felt as if I'd been falling asleep. The door slid open for her as she glided towards it.

'What's behind the door?' I said.

'Oh, that's the heartbeat of the Life Shop,' Simon said. 'The centre of operations. We call it the Pulse Room. It's where everything happens, where the decisions are made.'

'By Cassandra Catto?' I asked.

'She's one of our directors,' said Simon. 'She was one of the founders of the Life Shop.'

'Tevision,' said Charlie again.

'Yes, she's on television, isn't she, Charlie?' said Simon, but Charlie was pointing at somebody else by now. A fair-haired man in a dark suit was following Cassandra to the door with a quick, determined step.

'Trevor McLean!' I sat up straight. 'He's our MP!'

Something around Simon's eyes flickered, but he still smiled. 'He's very keen on visiting successful businesses,' he said. 'Sorry, Lorna, you're sitting in strong sunlight there. I'll turn the air conditioning your way.'

An electric fan was humming to itself from the wall, and he reached up to tilt it my way. I did feel better for it. I was still wondering about Trevor McLean but Simon was talking about Charlie, and amazing me with how much he knew about cerebral palsy. He told me all about the therapies the Life Shop could offer, free holidays, a lightweight buggy… it made such perfect sense that I couldn't help nodding as I listened. He could see every single one of our problems. Then I realized he'd asked me something and I was about to say yes, which wasn't very bright because I hadn't even heard the question.

'Sorry, can you run that by me again?' I said.

'I was asking you if Charlie's doing well with the vitamins we sent. We'd like to monitor his progress.'

'Oh, he's doing fine,' I said vaguely.

'Then he can see one of our medical team,' he said. 'They're all highly qualified and experienced doctors.'

I think I said Charlie had his own doctor, but I'm not sure what I said or whether I just jibbered at him. Through all that dozy fuzz in my head, a warning screamed.

Doctor. It triggered an alarm, jangled me, shook me up. I could have been drifting into sleep or a trance or something, saying 'yes' to everything, until that word 'doctor' set the sirens screeching. There was something about a doctor, something really important, if I could remember what it was.

Why was I here? I hadn't come all this way to soak up whatever Shiny Simon told me. I was here to find out something, if I could only remember what. But it was so pleasant just to watch the waterfall as the breeze from the air conditioning wafted music into me…

With a huge effort, I heaved Charlie onto my lap. He felt so heavy that for a moment I thought I wouldn't be able to move him, he seemed like a dense, heavy lump that would tear my arms from my sockets. I heaved so hard that my shoulders strained and ached. Then I settled him on my knee with my arms fastened round him so that Simon couldn't see what I did next.

I fastened my right hand round my left wrist, bit my lip, and dug my nails so hard into my skin that pain shot up my arm. That did it. I was wide awake and sharp again. I was here to find out what they were up to. What was Kieron doing?

'My friend came here to work during the summer,' I said. 'Kieron Miller.'

'Oh, Kieron!' he said. 'He's doing a great job, he's a real member of the team. Would you like to see him?'

Of course I would! But what if I said yes, allowing Simon to escort me to goodness knows where, taking Charlie with me? But if I said no, I'd go away without finding out anything about Kieron.

It wasn't like me to be so dithery. The Life Shop was getting to me.

'He's working in the Pulse Room,' he said. 'I can take you there to meet him. It'll be a great opportunity for you.' He stood up. 'Shall we go now?'

'I need to take Charlie to the loo,' I said. I couldn't think straight with Simon shadowing over me, and that was the only place where he couldn't come with me. I hauled Charlie off to the loo.

It was like the Millionaire Manor House Hotel in there, all gleaming peach sinks, pot pourri and scented soap, but I knew what they were up to. It was all part of soothing and cossetting visitors until they'd believe everything they were told.

I pulled myself together and splashed cold water on my face to keep myself sharp. I took Charlie to the loo, gave us both a good wash and tried to think of all the phrases

I'd heard. Suddenly it was as if they were spinning round
in my head:

We give you exactly what you want. Give you... Give...
No you don't, you sell it.
Kieron. Television. Doctor.
DOCTOR!
Doctor Faustus!

9

That's what *Dr Faustus* is about. He makes a pact with the devil so he can have all he wants, but he has to pay a price. He pays with his soul, and at the end his time runs out and the demons are waiting to drag him down to hell. It's about getting whatever you want, but you lose your soul. You can call it soul, spirit, identity, whatever you like, but that's what was happening at the Life Shop. You bought a whole new lifestyle and in return you became a mindless clone and it was happening everywhere – in homes, schools, workplaces, all over the country. I grabbed Charlie and hugged him as hard as I could.

'Charlie?' I said. He was always so contented, I couldn't tell whether they'd got him as dazed as everyone else. I snatched Peter Rabbit out of his hands and he gave me a look like murder and grabbed it back again. Good. Charlie was still himself.

They had some of those padded velvet chairs in there and I sat down, cuddling Charlie on my lap. Simon had offered to take me to the Pulse Room to see Kieron. If I did, I'd get to see what Kieron was doing, and what Trevor McLean had to do with all this. He was a senior member of the government, and if Simon expected me to believe he was only there for a chummy little visit he was insulting my intelligence. But I didn't want to take Charlie in there, and I didn't want to leave him in their crèche, either.

He planted a big wet kiss on my cheek. He does that when you're not expecting it, and I rocked him.

'I don't know, Charlie,' I said, thinking out loud. 'I don't know what to do.'

'What do,' said Charlie.

'What to do,' I repeated.

'Train,' said Charlie.

So one of us could still make a decision, and it sounded sensible to me. Charlie's safety was more important than Kieron, or anything else at that moment. Right, I thought. Train it is. The next problem was how to get out of the building without being stopped by Simon. I knew he'd be waiting outside, ready to take me to the Pulse Room. *Pulse Room.* Sounded like an operating theatre. I'd have to face him, but perhaps I could talk my way out, make excuses and go. I found Smiley Si waiting for us as near to the door of the ladies loo as a man can be without getting his face slapped.

'I'm afraid we have to go,' I said. 'We have to catch our train.'

'We booked you on to the 4.32, didn't we?' he said promptly. 'You've got lots of time. I'll tell them to order you a taxi to the station, make it easier for you.'

I went with him to the reception desk while he ordered a taxi. What else could I do? The urge to grab Charlie and run tore at me, telling me to snatch him up and dash for the door. But Charlie couldn't run, and I couldn't run far carrying him. I wouldn't have time to get hold of the wheelchair and get him into it – if I tried to escape, the automatic doors would lock before I got to them.

Of course they couldn't keep me there against my will, but I knew how clever the Life Shop was. They could say they were worried about me, sit me down, bring me a drink, sweep Charlie off to the crèche… after five minutes of sweet music and hypnotic air I'd be a hundred per cent gaga.

So much for getting Charlie out fast. I had no choice but to pick up the chair and go with Simon. At least this way I'd see Kieron, and I might even find out what was happening. And the other thing I'd find out was the quickest way out of the building, because by then I was terrified. I mustn't show it, but I was.

'May I have my brother's wheelchair, please?' I asked the receptionist.

'You won't need that, will you?' said Simon.

'He's tired,' I said, and he was, because he climbed into the chair the second he saw it. I was watching everything at once, glancing in every direction, noticing doors, windows, signs, desks, badges, adverts, displays, pinboards. I listened to voices, picking up snippets of conversation. I didn't learn much, but at least my brain had something to work on instead of soaking up the mushy music. We walked round the goldfish pool, and though I tried to stay calm my hands were clenched on that wheelchair by the time we reached the fake cliff. Smoothly and silently, the door slid open.

No more music. That was the first thing to strike me. Thank goodness that's over, I thought, but then I heard canned laughter and more music, loud and jangly. Just in front of me was a long table in semi-darkness because the people sitting there were watching a screen at the end of the room, like a cinema screen. They sat in a row with their backs to me and their heads tilted upwards as they watched. It was showing some daft game show – that explained the music – with a lumpy woman in a too-tight dress trying to juggle pomegranates and answer easy-peasy questions at the same time. The people at the table just watched without a flicker of anything, but laughter came from the soundtrack. It was the kind of brain-free zone that keeps everyone goggling at the telly on a Saturday night.

Below the screen was a stage, with ranks of state-of-the-art computers lined along the front, and two or three soundboards, the kind we use in school for drama. There were computers everywhere – on the stage, around the room, on the tables – all with screensavers flickering. The Pulse Room seemed to be a mixture of meeting room, cinema and high-tech recording studio. One thing that I couldn't identify at all stood pretty much in the centre of the room, between the table and the stage.

It was a black marble column, a plinth, standing a little taller than my waist. It looked as if there should be something on top of it, but there was nothing. Nothing. It stood quite alone, as if it waited for something, and I found I was staring at it.

It threatened me. Somehow it was like Darth Vader, or a bully in a playground, and I forced myself to look away and take in the rest of the room. Plain grey high-tech, that was all. A room with no windows, and probably soundproof.

Oh, please, get me out of this place, I thought, but this was what I'd come for. Would I have been brave enough to go there if Simon hadn't made me? To this day, I don't know. But now I was there, I had to hold my nerve and see the thing through. Or try to.

The game show finished, the sound faded, and the screen blanked. The silence as the film ended was as threatening as a growling dog, and in it I could hear something like a heartbeat. It might have been my own, I was so scared.

'That will go out at weekend prime time with our adverts slotted in at twenty-minute intervals,' said somebody at the table. 'Plus flash messages.' They all murmured approvingly, then Simon said, a touch too loudly and quickly, that he'd brought a visitor.

'This is Lorna,' he said. 'And Charlie.'

The talk stopped as if they'd been switched off. Every head at that table turned to look at us. I smiled politely, and so did they. I didn't recognize them all, but of course there was Cassandra Catto, looking even more stunning than on telly, with Trevor McLean next to her.

There was a huge, red-faced man I'd seen on the news the week before, so I knew he was a top-rank policeman. There was a television executive who'd been on the news, too, because he'd just taken over a big satellite network, and a woman who'd won an international journalism award – she'd been to talk to our sixth form. I didn't recognize the rest until I saw pictures of them afterwards, but how many judges, MPs and army chiefs would you recognize if you passed them in the street? Then Cassandra Catto gave me the chummiest smile, as if she were my auntie.

'Lovely to meet you both,' she said. 'Not many visitors see this room. You must have impressed Simon.'

'Lorna's given me a hard time all afternoon,' said Simon. 'She asks tough questions.'

'Good,' said Cassandra, and I felt the look that passed

between them. 'Lorna, you're very welcome. In this room, all our Life Shop decisions are made. I hope you're happy with the service you get from us?'

'I don't get any,' I said. 'I'm not a customer.'

'But her mum is a very good client,' said Simon. He tapped at the nearest computer and read from the screen. 'Latest order placed 31 July. Insurance payment, query about home employment for the Life Shop. I hope she joins the team. Ordered T-shirts, trousers, complimentary pack of children's vitamins, and… oh, I'd better not read out the next bit, Lorna. It might be for your birthday.'

'But I don't…' I began, and stopped. If I said, 'I don't want anything from your catalogue', they'd gang up.

'I get the impression,' said Cassandra gently, 'that you are one of those customers whose needs are simply not being met, and that isn't good enough. If we're not delivering what you want, Lorna, we're letting you down.'

'It's cool. There's nothing I want,' I said. 'Except I'd like to know who you all are. Are you all directors?'

'Oh, yes,' she said, 'and we come from all walks of life.' She was so warm and kind, she was almost holding my hand. I hoped she was going to introduce me personally to the Society of Big Cheeses, but Simon handed her a print-out from the computer and her eyebrows shot into her hairline. I tried to see what she was reading, but all I could make out was my name.

'What a high flier you are, Lorna!' she said. 'Where do

you plan to go to university?'

'I haven't thought that far ahead,' I said.

'Looking at your academic record, there's no reason why you shouldn't go to Oxford or Cambridge,' she said. 'And I know...' she drew me away from the others and lowered her voice. 'If you don't mind me mentioning it, I know money can be a problem. You need to get a savings plan started, immediately. It doesn't have to be with us, of course, though we do offer an excellent policy.'

'Money never used to be a problem,' I said loudly, though it wasn't strictly true. I turned round so the others could hear me. 'Money was OK until my mum got into debt with you.'

I could see Simon ready to come in with his 'debt isn't debt' line, but Cassandra silenced him with a look.

'Oh, if we arranged a student savings plan with you we'd cancel the interest on your mum's account,' she said, as if it wasn't worth a second thought. 'No problem. And here's little Charlie. I wonder what we can do for him?'

Charlie had fallen asleep in his wheelchair. He looked pink and helpless. Peter Rabbit's ear was soggy where he'd been sucking it.

'Poor Charlie,' she said softly, as she bent over him. She looked up at me with a kind, motherly face, and I had to remind myself that she was used to playing for the cameras. 'What's going to happen to him when your mum can't look after him any more?'

'I'll look after him,' I said. I knelt to rearrange him in the chair so he could be comfortable, and she knelt down, too, beside me.

'Of course you will,' she said. 'You want the best for Charlie. Please, Lorna, accept our help for him. He can have the best consultant in the world.'

'He's got that,' I said, but she didn't stop.

'He can have a full life. He can grow up strong and normal, able to look after himself. If you let us help, we can arrange everything he needs.'

If only it was true, if only I was wrong about the Life Shop... I looked into her eyes and saw the mascara and liner, and the practised look of an actress. What could they do that Dr Montgomery couldn't?

'Why?' I challenged her. 'Why are you so concerned about Charlie?'

'Because we want the best,' she said earnestly. 'The best for everyone. The Life Shop is about quality of life, the best quality of life, for everyone.'

My hands were shaking, but I looked her in the eyes. 'If they can pay for it,' I said.

She dropped her voice and spoke reassuringly, like a mother. This was between Cassandra and me.

'It's never more than you can pay, Lorna,' she purred. 'You may think you can't afford what we offer, but I promise you, you can.'

I could at least find out more about it. I remembered the blurb in their catalogue – I could always cancel with twenty-eight days' notice. I pictured a team of top-flight medics gathered round Charlie, and how much it would cost, and if the Life Shop would pay... then the thought of money and doctors made me think of Dr Faustus again. They'd nearly caught me. When I realized how close I'd come to giving in, I tell you, I was so scared I thought I might be sick.

I'd been there far too long. I jumped up and yanked the chair round so hard that Charlie woke up and squealed, and I charged that wheelchair at the door.

It didn't open. I spun round and faced Simon.

'Let me out,' I demanded.

'Please, Lorna,' said a voice behind me. 'Please, Lorna, don't go. Not now.'

It was a familiar voice, and in that strange, shut-in place it was so welcome, more welcome than it had ever been! I whirled round.

'Kieron!' I said. Then I saw his face, and the hope drained out of me.

10

He still looked like Kieron, but I looked into his eyes and couldn't find him. I saw someone who would never question a teacher's judgment, never ask difficult questions, or try a new idea just to see if it worked. Someone who wasn't quite alive. But he was laughing.

'Lorna, what's the matter?' he said, as if it wasn't obvious. 'This place is fantastic! I never dreamed it would be this good, I've done so much. Did you see that preview? I was behind the camera for that. I'm working in here today.' He turned to show me a camera that looked like a small robot. 'They let me use that. I'm filming parts of the board meeting for a "behind-the-scenes" DVD. They've offered me a training scheme and sponsorship, and a full-time job as soon as I want it.'

So this was what had happened to Kieron. Could it happen to me? They were all round me with Kieron grinning smugly down at me, and I wanted to slap his silly face.

'And you're the kind we want to recruit, too, Lorna,' said Cassandra Catto. 'We'd do the same for you, as part of your further education programme.'

'Go for it,' urged Kieron. 'You should. You'll never get such a good opportunity again.'

That hurt. I went for him. 'Oh, won't I?' I snapped. 'Do you take me for a no-hoper? I can make my own opportunities without a glossy catalogue and a posh camera. I'll get into university and I'll go places, and I'll do it the way I always have, by working hard, and you'd think the same way yourself if you hadn't been taken in by all this hype. Is that camera running? Are you filming this? Well, don't cut the next bit, because it's the best.'

I moved in closer to him, and he took a tiny step back. The directors had formed a half circle around me, and I felt it drawing tighter.

'Kieron Miller just sold out,' I snapped. 'Sold his soul for – what's that camera worth? It's not even yours, Kieron, they only let you play with it. Do they give you a nice studio to work in? A big shiny playroom? You're pathetic. Now, let me out. I'm going.'

I wheeled the chair at the door, but Simon and Kieron stood shoulder to shoulder in front of it.

'Excuse me,' I said, but they didn't move, and for sheer fury I drove that chair straight at Kieron's ankles to make him get out of the way – only he didn't. He must have thought I wouldn't really do it. He stumbled forwards with a gasp of pain, nearly landing right on top of the wheelchair so that I was scared for Charlie and ducked to wrap myself round him, but as Kieron fell he overbalanced the other way, and the chair lurched but didn't tip over. There was a crash and a shout and I knew Kieron must have got really hurt, because mostly he doesn't swear. Something hit the floor.

I looked up from the wheelchair. A file had fallen off the table, with papers and photos falling out everywhere. I don't know how long it took – it can't have been long – but on the pictures and notes scattered across the carpet, I saw all I needed to know.

There were shots from the film I'd just seen, but these were different. They had the word 'subliminals' stamped across them, and there were touches in those pictures I hadn't seen in the bright, silly game show, phrases printed across the pictures: *'Love the Life Shop.' 'The Life Shop is happiness.'* Some had 'signature tune' stamped on them.

I knew what 'subliminal' meant. It means slipping a message into your subconscious so quickly that you don't know you're picking it up. There were passport photos of the people on the board, too, and their names – I didn't get it all, but it was 'General Somebody', 'Lady Whatsherface', and one of them was a high-court judge.

I'd taken all this in before I turned to see if Charlie was

OK, but he was fine, gazing into space and waving Peter Rabbit around. Trevor McLean was doing his 'MP and baby' routine, wiggling his fingers at him.

'Leave him alone,' I said. 'We're leaving.'

'Lorna, my dear,' said Cassandra kindly. 'You really must stay.'

The half circle had closed into a ring. They were all round us with no way out, no gaps. Kieron was one of them. He was nursing his hand – he must have hurt it when he fell – and I really hoped he'd fractured something. Sorry, but I did.

'You really must stay,' said Cassandra again, and she stepped towards me from her place in the circle. The gap closed behind her. 'You know far too much now.'

I'd thought I was scared before. Oh, how wrong I'd been.

11

'It's all right.' She was like a kindly nurse, calming me down before an operation. 'Don't be afraid, Lorna, nobody's going to harm you. You want an explanation about the Life Shop, and that's what I'll give you.'

Like a frightened little kid I just wanted to go home, but I wasn't saying so. Not to them. Even if I did, they wouldn't have let me out. I'd have to go along with things for the moment, co-operate, stay sharp and guard Charlie with my life. At the first half chance that came, I'd trick my way out.

'You're a bright girl,' she said. 'You know the Life Shop is more than a mail-order service, and you're right. You know we influence people's lives, the way they think, the decisions they make. Yes, we do. We want to change the world. Don't you think the world needs changing?'

'Yes,' I said, 'but not like this.'

'Yes,' she repeated. 'Is it safe to be out at night on your own? Are the cities safe? Think about all the violent crime, all over the world. The Life Shop makes people feel contented. If they're contented, why bother to be aggressive? We're promoting a peaceful society.'

There was a good answer to that, but for the moment I couldn't think of it. The place was getting to me again.

'Is there a drug problem in your school?' she said, and I think I must have said yes. She was leading the way to the front of the stage and I followed her without thinking, wheeling Charlie in front of me. The circle parted to let us through, and formed again around us. Somebody must have dimmed the lights. I could hear that heartbeat again, like a tuneless drum.

'Nobody wants drugs when they have the Life Shop,' she said. 'They don't need them. They're satisfied.'

It was as if my blood was turning grey and sluggish inside me. Whatever it was doing it can't have been taking oxygen or anything else to my brain, because my brain only wanted to sleep. Arguing was a huge effort, and I struggled to do it.

'Content?' I said. 'Mum isn't. She's working twenty-five hours a day to pay you.'

'She chose to make a credit arrangement,' she said gently. 'Our clients always have a choice, and she can easily clear her account. We'll make it so easy for her.'

'Only by persuading her to work for you,' I said, but I

didn't like saying it. It seemed so ungrateful to this kind woman who was taking so much trouble to explain everything.

'But isn't it wonderful that there's so much work available!' she said. 'The Life Shop is so big, and getting bigger. We can provide lots of employment, including work from home for people who have family commitments. We offer training and education, to help people like your mother move on and have the career they've always wanted. What they've always dreamed of.'

Oh. I'd never thought of that. I didn't want to come between Mum and her dreams, I hadn't meant to be selfish. Her life had been hard before the Life Shop. How could I begrudge it to her?

We sat down a few feet away from that black column thing. It looked as if it should have a bird bath or something on top. The heartbeat sound was stronger.

I struggled to remember what I was there for. Dreams. She'd said something about dreams. Come on, Lorna, pull yourself together. What was my friend's name again? Thingy's sister. Oh, yes.

'Fern,' I said. 'My friend Fern, she had a dream. She wanted to run her own restaurant one day, and she had loads of ideas about it. She was always laughing. Now she just looks glazed and talks about fast-food outlets.'

'Yes, we know about her,' said Cassandra. 'Fern's a sweet girl, but really, she doesn't have your intellect. She has no idea of the hard work and risks of running a restaurant, or the responsibility. Much better this way.'

'But she should have the chance to find out!' I argued. 'It's her choice! You said all your customers have choice!'

'Yes, and Fern has chosen our way,' she said calmly. 'So has Kieron.'

I couldn't concentrate with all those eyes watching me. All those important people couldn't be wrong, surely? What made me think that Lorna Young of Hutton Park was right, and everybody else from the Secretary of State downwards had got it wrong?

The Secretary of State.

'Just a minute,' I said, and looked round at them. The media. The government. The police, the army, the law… between them, they could take over the country. Trevor McLean had done a computer deal abroad. Did that include software? How much power can you have, if you influence the world of computers? Then I knew for certain that it wasn't my own pulse I could hear, because what I was hearing was a slow, steady beat and my heart was racing, fast and hard. I wanted to run.

'Oh, yes,' said Cassandra. She seemed to know what I was thinking. 'We're not there yet, but we will be. We will be invincible. The police, the government, the law, the media, the medical profession, education, computer experts, they are all gathering to us. Won't it be wonderful if they all stop arguing and work together? And they will, when they give us their hearts and minds.'

Well, you're not having mine, I thought, and found my old fighting self again. 'And you'll turn them into zombies?' I said. 'Like all your staff?'

'Zombies?' she said. 'Do you see zombies? I see pleasant, co-operative people who are happy in their work. The Life Shop is about making life simple.'

I thought of the subliminal messages. 'But you've got them practically hypnotized!' I cried.

'Oh, no,' she said. 'Everyone has a choice.'

I hadn't. I wanted to get out. I reminded myself to co-operate while I looked for a chance to trick them.

'What choice do I have?' I said.

'Whatever you want,' she said. 'Choose your dreams.'

All I wanted to choose was the 4.32 from Pellmarket Station, but I was too far in for that. I'd seen how these creeps were spreading their tendrils through the country – the world, probably – and I had to do something. Nobody else would. If only I could concentrate, it would help.

'Have you found Lorna's file on the computer, Kieron?' said Cassandra. 'Video link it, please.'

I tried to guess what they had on my file, but I was distracted by something happening to the black column. Out of the corner of my eye I'd seen a flicker of colour and light wriggle across the top. Something was happening. I watched it to see if it would happen again, then looked away in case it was giving me subliminal messages or something. My name flashed up on the screen:

LORNA YOUNG! WELCOME TO YOUR DREAMS.

'I don't want to see this,' I snapped.

'Oh, Lorna,' said Cassandra gently. 'You're so hurt and angry.'

'Don't give me that,' I said. Music began, but it wasn't their sort of music. It was the end of Sibelius's Second Symphony, and that's one of my most favourite pieces in all the world. Do you know it? It's stirring and wonderful, and when I hear it I feel I can do anything. As I soaked up the Sibelius, the film began.

To this day, I'm not sure what I watched. It looked like me, but it wasn't me. I think it was was one of those very good animations that almost looks real. I saw myself, playing the piano in a band, playing the organ in a cathedral, then as a concert soloist in one of those gorgeous ballgowns. And I looked great, even better than Fern does, so good that I wanted to stop it and freeze the frames. I needn't be the 'plain-but-brainy' one, the one always hidden behind Charlie's wheelchair, the one making do. I'd wear a deep red ballgown and play to a packed concert hall and Dad would queue up in the rain for a ticket to hear me. Everyone would gaze in admiration at Lorna Young.

I saw myself at university with a bunch of friends, all laughing and talking and going places together, then going forward in a black academic gown to get my degree, with everyone congratulating me and Mum so proud and happy that it made me cry. I didn't want to cry in front of Cassandra Catto, but honestly, I couldn't help it.

I was seeing dreams I never knew I had. I glimpsed what life might be if we weren't always thinking about Charlie's wheelchair, Charlie's exercises and Charlie's diet, and there'd be more time for me. When I saw myself at university, I was so popular! With all those friends, I'd never again mind that my own father didn't want to stay with me. I'd be free from everything that ever hurt.

Yes. In my heart, I was already saying it. *Yes.* I knew there was a good reason for saying *no*, but all that I'd seen – the music, the university, the applause, the popularity, the freedom – it was a craving like hunger, no, like starving. All I had to do was claim it.

She was watching me. I knew I didn't want to let her win, even if I'd forgotten why not. Something stubborn inside me still resisted her, and I clawed my arm again while I tried to remember why I was there. Something to do with Fern, who was no fun any more, and the mindless look on Kieron's face…

I'd got the plot back again. The girl on that screen wasn't real.

'She isn't really me,' I said. I felt dizzy, as if I was talking to somebody far off who couldn't hear me, but I went on. 'Look at her eyes! It's just computer graphics! She's not real!'

'But you could…' began Cassandra, but I was determined not to listen.

'You don't really give a choice,' I said. 'You give a range, a set of options, and that's not the same thing. That's all you are, just a mail-order company. You tell us we can choose this one, that one, or the other one. You can have pink, mauve or black. Basic or de luxe. Fern can have a restaurant, but it won't be her choice or her dream. It'll be what you offer, and that isn't much. You can't offer anything half as good as the dream she has in her head.'

She'd so nearly caught me. I was angry with her and angrier with myself, because again I'd nearly fallen for it. And as for Kieron… I rounded on him.

'You know, I always thought your mum ordered you two from a catalogue,' I said. 'You're both so perfect. Well, the best things in life don't come out of catalogues. You don't get people like me out of catalogues. I'm so stroppy not even my father wants me, and what's more, I don't care. And you don't get kids like Charlie out of catalogues, because who'd order one like him? Nobody would want him, but let me tell you, all of you, he is the most wonderful thing that ever happened to me and he is priceless and beautiful in a way you'll never understand, because you've all got catalogues where your hearts should be.'

Suddenly I'd run out of things to say, and I was exhausted. I turned on Cassandra. 'Satisfied?' I said.

Now she'll be angry, I thought. She stayed as cool as a fountain. She didn't even attempt to deny anything.

'That's all right,' she said sweetly. 'Nobody will force you to accept anything. So what about Charlie?'

I pulled his chair towards me, and my hand felt weak and shaky. Charlie stirred at the sound of his name and made little disgruntled noises, but he stayed put.

The circle around me was tighter and closer. I didn't have to look round to know that. I could feel it. The heartbeat was louder. Flickers of blue and green light licked over the top of the black plinth like a hungry tongue.

'Don't be afraid, Lorna,' said Cassandra gently. 'Look. Only look at this one last video.'

I didn't want to look at the screen, but I couldn't help it. I watched a little boy like Charlie, but not like Charlie. He was in a classroom with other children, listening, writing in his workbook, stretching up his hand to answer questions. I saw him kick a football around, and go bowling. I saw him with no sticks, running down hills, hurling himself into swimming pools, scrambling over rocks, just being a boy.

'With our care and our course of treatment,' she said, 'this is what Charlie can be.'

'You can't do anything Dr Montgomery can't do,' I said, but I was shaking. I'd seen what Charlie could be like without his disability. It was so beautiful.

'Of course we couldn't!' she cried. 'We'd be working *with* Dr Montgomery! He can't possibly provide the best treatment if he doesn't have funding! We'd sponsor Charlie's treatment.'

That wasn't fair. If Charlie could get sponsorship, what about all the disabled children who couldn't? Wasn't it hard on them? But I could still see the little brother on the screen.

'We'd have to start at once,' she said. 'There's no time to lose.'

Whatever I'd seen and heard and thought that day, I'd forgotten it. All I could think of was Charlie. If I went on fighting the Life Shop, I was shutting the door on all hope for Charlie. We'd always made sacrifices for him. What was so different about this? And really, this wasn't even a sacrifice. I'd decided to be difficult and fight them, but here I was, fighting the people who wanted to help us.

'What do I have to do?' I said.

She nodded at somebody. A printer purred. I knelt down to talk to Charlie, because he was getting restless. When the printer stopped, someone handed Cassandra a document and she laid it neatly on the black plinth with a silver pen beside it.

'There's your agreement, Lorna,' she said. 'Read it as carefully as you like. We promise to provide you with a music scholarship at university, with travel and grooming allowance. We guarantee to cancel all your mother's debt to us. Charlie will have the best treatment money can buy, anywhere in the world, with Dr Montgomery or another consultant of your choice. You promise to say nothing of anything you've seen here, but we can guarantee that you won't want to. You will shop from our catalogue on very favourable terms, and will agree to let us guide your career in the way we think is most suitable. You will take part in the Life Shop's projects and advertising as required.'

The contract waited for me. I had to read it, but it was as if it was printed in my mind already, like a song I'd always known. Dimly, I remembered my arguments against the Life Shop. *You don't have real choice, you can only choose what they offer.* But what they were offering Charlie was good enough.

There was a movement beside me and I must have known it was Charlie climbing out of the chair, but I didn't look. I didn't even check on where he was going.

It isn't free, you have to pay for it. I had to pay with my whole future, and be on their side.

The words were heavy. I had to force them through. 'You want my soul,' I said.

There was gentle laughter around me. 'I beg your pardon?' said Cassandra.

'My soul, my heart, my life,' I said. 'That's want you want, isn't it?' It was clearer now. 'That's what you do with the people who buy from you. You steal their souls!'

'Oh, Lorna!' said Cassandra sweetly, as if she was talking to a toddler. 'How can anyone take a soul? And what would we do with one?'

They all laughed, but the answer was staring me in the face. I mean *really* staring me in the face as I looked down at the plinth, except I didn't look *at* it, I looked *into* it. All the way down as far as I could see it was hollow, much too narrow to fall down, but it was as if you *could* fall down it and never get out. My hands tingled. I wondered how it worked, what fuelled it, and what was so important about it. Touching it, I felt that heartbeat as if it were seeking my own heart, pulling me in. Though I couldn't remember picking it up, the silver pen was in my hand.

Over the top of the plinth I saw two long furry ears and something that was blue, something familiar. It was so ridiculous that for a moment I thought the whole thing was a dream and I'd wake up. But the plinth was real, the pulse and the flashing lights were real, the pen was real, and that was Charlie's Peter Rabbit appearing over the edge – Peter Rabbit, clutched in one little fist, then the other hand appeared over the edge, then the top of Charlie's head because he was pulling himself up, stretching over to see what I was doing...

'No!' I screamed, and as his big blue eyes appeared over the top I grabbed him to drag him away from that horrible black mouth. 'No, Charlie, don't touch it!'

I heaved him from the plinth, he struggled against me, the contract fell on the floor, and he dropped Peter Rabbit. I saw it tumble down helplessly into the heart of the black plinth.

The noise was appalling. Below Charlie's howls, sounds of grinding and groaning came from deep beneath the plinth, grim and horrible like a roaring monster. Around me the directors shrieked and gasped, but more than anything, above their cries and the growling of the plinth, I heard Charlie sobbing unbearably for his toy.

I need to tell you exactly what happened, but that slows it down and it only took a few seconds. The decision itself wasn't even a second, only a breath, but it was the most vital breath of my life. I didn't know what was down that plinth, I only knew that Charlie's toy was down there – and I knew that I was young and healthy and all in one piece, and I wanted to stay that way.

The only thing to do was the worst thing to do. I turned my face away and plunged my arm down the plinth. I already knew how stupid it was. Stupid, stupid thing to do! At any moment my fingers could be grabbed or ground to shreds, or my arm could be ripped off; somehow I'd found the courage to do it, but it was wearing off fast and I was terrified. I couldn't feel the toy, and I only wanted my arm out before it got mangled or the rest of me was dragged in, too. Oh, please, please, get me out. I was panicking, sweating, wishing I hadn't done it – then my fingers touched fur, and with all my strength I wrenched at it.

Some force was pulling against me but I kept heaving, praying that Peter Rabbit would come out in one piece. Never mind Peter Rabbit, I wanted my arm out of there, fast, before that thing could crunch it, digest it or turn it to stone. At any moment it might start, and then... but nothing at all was happening to me. It wasn't hurting.

I could hear music, snatches and fragments of things that I'd never heard before, coming from inside the plinth. From that horrible thing I was hearing stunning, beautiful music, a few bars of something, then it faded and changed to something new. Even as I heaved at the toy I was taking in the tantalizing music, and wanting more. My eyes were closed, but behind them I could see pictures as bright and breathtaking as the music, vivid and real, changing all the time so I couldn't take in each one. I'd never seen such life and joy in pictures. I could feel laughter, not hear it, but feel it. Laughter and excitement were whirling around me, and with them came a rushing sensation like flying. If I'd thought about it, I might have thought it was worth losing my arm for, but I wasn't thinking about that any more – I was still pulling, but I'd stopped being afraid. Like flying...

Then I lost my balance.

12

I lost my balance because the rabbit came free so suddenly that I crashed over backwards. Kieron shouted my name. Charlie stopped screaming and snatched Peter Rabbit from me. The plinth juddered and shook. Around me there were pathetic little cries as the directors gasped and whimpered. Sirens screeched. Alarms rang. Footsteps were running from somewhere, and Kieron was pulling me to my feet.

'Run!' he said.

I grabbed Charlie, Kieron took the wheelchair, and we dashed for the doors. Kieron banged an emergency button on the wall so that the doors slid open; they began shutting again immediately, but Kieron turned, rammed the chair between them to wedge them open, and held out his arms.

I was glancing over my shoulder as I lifted Charlie to

him. I thought they'd all be running after us, but they weren't. They couldn't. Cassandra Catto was curled up on the floor whimpering, Trevor McLean stood there shaking with his mouth open; two of the others were clinging to each other. The rest were stumbling towards the plinth as if it were driftwood from a shipwreck.

'Get out, Lorna!' yelled Kieron, and nearly dragged me over the wheelchair before he yanked it free and the doors banged together. We pushed Charlie into it, strapped him in and ran.

Kieron led the way across the car park. A barrier was coming down, but we ducked under, tipping the chair back to get Charlie through, and went on running until I couldn't breathe, my side hurt and I had to stop. We hid in the shelter of a wall while I got my breath back.

'What's going on?' I gasped.

'You OK?' he asked. He was breathless, too.

'What's happened to you all of a sudden?' I said. 'Were you faking?'

'What?' said Kieron unhelpfully.

'I don't get it,' I said. I was still a bit out of breath. 'Ten minutes ago, you were a zombie. Were you faking?'

He shook his head. 'They had me,' he said. 'I believed it all. I'd taken it all in. There was nothing to argue about, it seemed so right.'

I looked around. Nobody seemed to have followed us. We started walking fast, but I had no idea where we were.

'Do you know your way around?' I said.

'No problem,' said Kieron. 'You'd better get to the station. How long before your train goes?'

I looked at my watch, and couldn't believe it. How long had we been in there? 'We've only got fifteen minutes!'

'Cool,' said Kieron. 'We'll make it. Keep walking.'

'So what happened to you?' I said. For a while he didn't reply, and I think he was still half in shock.

'I became like the rest of them,' he said at last. 'They had me, mind and heart, like you said. After a few days in there I still wanted to make tapes and films but I didn't want to experiment any more. I'd forgotten all my own ideas, I just wanted to do what they suggested. I enjoyed it, in a bland sort of way. I never had to make decisions, and if anything went wrong it wasn't my responsibility. It was dead cushy. They fixed me up with a nice place to stay, the food was good, I got paid… I was so well looked after I didn't have to make an effort about anything.'

If we did that with Charlie, it was called over-protecting. But I didn't think it was the right time to say so.

'I don't think I even realized it,' he went on, still hurrying. 'It was like when you go through some weird phase, but you don't realize there's anything weird about it until later. Then you knocked me flying, and I fell and hit my wrist against the sharp edge of the table so hard I thought I'd broken it.'

'Sorry,' I said, and looked at his arm. There was a whacking great red weal on his wrist.

'No, it's cool,' he said. 'It hurt like hell, but it woke me up. Suddenly I couldn't understand what I was doing there, and whose side I was supposed to be on. I watched you and listened, and remembered. I went through all that when I first came here, working out what they were up to and then… I don't know.'

He frowned a bit, and I knew how he felt. I was confused myself. The sirens were still screeching, but they were further away.

'At some time or other,' he said, 'they offered me the world, and I must have said yes. Then I saw the same thing happening to you, but I didn't know how to make it stop.'

'Charlie made it stop,' I said. 'But I don't know exactly what happened.'

'I'm not sure how he did it,' he said, 'but he crippled the Pulse. That black thing, that's the Pulse – the power at the centre of the Life Shop. He dropped that rabbit down it and it jammed. It couldn't cope. With any luck it's given itself a breakdown. I only hope it can't be mended.'

We came to a main road and a police car shot past us with screaming sirens. Then another flew by with its lights flashing.

'They must have their security system linked to the police station,' said Kieron. Two wailing ambulances swerved round the corner. 'And the ambulance service,' he added.

I stopped walking. Kieron stopped and turned to face me with a frown of impatience on his face.

'What's the matter?' he said.

'We have to go back,' I said. 'I don't want to, we don't know what we'll walk into. But we just ran and left all those people like gibbering wrecks. Whatever they've done, they're still human, they're still people. We should go back and help. We can't just leave them.'

'Yeah, I know,' he said, but he turned and went striding on so that I had to scuttle along with the wheelchair to keep up. 'That's why I'm going back as soon as you're on the train.'

I stopped again.

'Oh, come on, Lorna!' said Kieron.

'I should go back too,' I said. 'I started it.' But I knew it wouldn't work, not with Charlie there, and anyway, Kieron went on walking.

'I don't want you going back there alone,' I said, but I was still hurrying along beside him to the station. He was right. If I'd come to Pellmarket alone there'd be nothing to stop me going back into that madhouse with Kieron. But there was Charlie to think of, and no way could I take him back in there.

'I'm sorry,' I said, and I really did feel bad about it. 'I've made the mess and you have to clear it up.'

'You did the right thing,' said Kieron. I could see signs to the station now. We weren't going the way I'd come, but Kieron obviously knew where he was going. 'What you have to do now is to get Charlie out of here. And something else, too.'

'Yes?' I said.

He glanced over his shoulder and walked closer to me. 'You were right about them stealing lives, or personalities, or souls, or whatever you want to call it,' he said. 'Of course, they don't explain it to you, but I worked it out. Whenever anyone makes a commitment to the Life Shop, by placing an order or signing any sort of arrangement with them, that's it. Somehow their life, who they really are, is channelled into the Pulse. The more you commit to, the more you buy, the more you get into debt, the more it takes from you, and whatever it takes gets transformed into the energy the Life Shop needs to keep going.'

'So,' I said, 'if it's drained life out of people, can they ever get it back?'

He smiled, really smiled his own dazzling smile, for the first time that day.

'Well, I'm OK, aren't I?' he said.

I wasn't sure if he was OK to stay, but I wasn't going to worry him by saying so. We were nearly at the station, and there was something I still wanted to understand.

'When my arm went down there,' I said, 'I thought it

would suck me in or something, but it was lovely – or it would have been, if I hadn't been scared of losing my arm. I heard music and saw paintings – just fragments of things, but they were wonderful.'

'They'd be part of somebody's dreams,' said Kieron thoughtfully. 'Dreams that hadn't been recycled yet.'

'If dreams went to be minced up in the plinth, how can anyone get them back?' I asked, but I don't think he knew because he didn't answer, just kept striding along with his face tense and fixed.

'What do you think the Pulse is doing now?' I asked as we reached the pedestrian crossing. 'What have we done?'

He shrugged. 'I'll find out when I go back,' he said.

What? The light turned green, but I didn't move.

'You're not going anywhere near the Pulse, are you?' I said. 'You're just going to see if they're OK?'

'You'll miss your train,' he said.

'Kieron!' I still didn't move, though Charlie pointed and waved his arms to tell me he'd seen the green man on the lights. 'You're free now! Go back, check that nobody's hurt and get out before it falls apart! Come home!'

'You've missed your light,' he said. When it changed again he took my arm and steered us over the crossing. Cheek! I would have protested, but there were more important things to argue about.

'Calm down, you're not in a movie,' he said. 'Besides, if I'm clearing out, I have to pack first.'

I wheeled the chair through the station entrance, and a waft of cool air met us. Something nagged at me to make sure Kieron was all right, but against it was the urge, the wild, desperate urge to run at the nearest train, ram the wheelchair onto it and get out fast.

'Is your room…' I began.

'It's nowhere near the Life Shop,' he said. 'It's near here.'

'Don't go there,' I said. 'If they're getting their act back together at the Life Shop, they'll be after you. They'll be waiting for you at your flat. Don't go there!'

'I have to,' he said. 'I'm not leaving all my stuff behind.'

'Come back another day, then,' I said. 'When we know it's safe.'

'You'll miss your train,' he said.

'Train!' said Charlie, but I'd already looked at the information board.

'It's running late,' I said.

'Good,' said Kieron, and moved us into a corner near to the coffee stall. I think he was keeping us out of the way of the security cameras, because he glanced round, reached deftly into the back pocket of his jeans and slipped an envelope into my hand.

'Take this,' he said, and added quickly, 'and don't open it. It's the card from a digital camera. When I got hurt and

113

came to my senses, I kept filming what was happening to you. Then when it dawned on me that we might have to escape, I slipped it out and sealed it. If you don't hear from me tomorrow, you make use of it. Got it?'

'Stupid nerd,' I said, and tucked the envelope into my bag. 'The first chance you get, phone me. Send me a text. But do something, and don't let them get hold of you again.'

'I'll be home soon,' he said, and I knew there was no point in asking what he meant by 'soon'. 'I'm not afraid of the Life Shop. I'm not running away.'

'Text me,' I said. 'And take care. Promise.'

'Sure,' he said, but he wasn't listening. He came with us to help get the wheelchair and everything loaded up. As the train glided onto the platform and I undid the harness, Charlie twisted round, gave Kieron that bright, beautiful smile with his eyes shining like magic and said, 'I going on *train!*'

I held out. I didn't cry until Kieron had gone.

People on trains prefer not to notice if you're crying. I settled Charlie on my knee and looked hard out of the window so I wouldn't embarrass anyone. And all the time Charlie was gazing out, saying 'sheep' and 'cows' and all that, and laughing when another train went by, and nothing could have made him so happy, not even if the Life Shop had given him the world.

The carriage was warm and we were both hot, sticky and uncomfortable by the time we were getting home, but Charlie was still happy and still saying his sentence. I got all the bags and stuff together and heaved the chair out from between the seats. Well, it stuck, didn't it? It's a great big brute of a thing and it must have got wedged or something, and it's hard to fight with a stuck wheelchair when you've got your brother and a lifetime's supply of luggage in the other hand. A man who was getting up at the same time moved in to give me a hand. He tugged the chair and it still stuck, so he gave it such a heave I was afraid he'd wreck it. It shot out all of a sudden and crashed into a table where a young woman was looking at a magazine. The jolt knocked it right out of her hands, and as I saw it my legs went wobbly.

It wasn't a magazine, it was the Life Shop catalogue. The colours hit me. I saw Cassandra Catto's grinning face, looking so alive that she seemed to be laughing at me, and my stomach lurched. The catalogue slithered to the floor and landed right at my feet and I shot back before it could touch me. I knew I should pick it up, but I couldn't, I swear to you, I could have put my hand in the fire sooner than touch that catalogue.

The man was in front of me, the woman was beside me, the queue was behind me – I couldn't move! Clutching Charlie's hand, keeping him close to me, I turned hot and cold. I was trapped. Charlie was there, the catalogue was there, and I was in a nightmare. All these people must be from the Life Shop, ready to drag us back… I couldn't scream. I couldn't even breathe.

'Are you all right?' said the man, but he was looking at the woman at the table, not me. He picked up the catalogue and plonked it back in front of her.

'No problem,' she said, and pushed it away across the table. 'I wasn't bothered about it.'

So they weren't the Life Shop's spies! She didn't even care about the catalogue! Did that mean the Life Shop was losing its grip? With a rush of hope I wheeled Charlie across the platform and felt lighter, as if the sun had come out after a thunderstorm. I wanted to share the happiness with Charlie, so I bought him a little Thomas the Tank Engine flag from a stall on the platform and he waved it all the way to the bus.

But in the melting heat of the packed-full bus, I relived the afternoon. The grey room and the Pulse haunted me. Heaven only knew what the Pulse was doing now. It might have escaped from the plinth and be spreading its cloud all over the country. And what if they'd gone after Kieron and caught him? I held on tightly to my bag, to keep his card as close and safe as I could. I couldn't keep him safe, but it was the next best thing.

And if the Life Shop really was destroyed, what would happen to all the people who lived, ate, slept and breathed for it? Were they addicted? Would they go through terrible withdrawal symptoms? Cassandra Catto's smile glinted down at me from a poster and it was as if she could see into my bag and was laughing at me.

It had been a long day. My feet hurt, and I wished I had a drink. It was all right for Charlie, who'd fallen asleep almost as soon as we got on the bus, but there was still the long plod home from the bus stop at the other end. The bus was packed and the chair was too big for the luggage rack, so it got into everyone's way. Charlie sprawled across my lap, pink and snoring and all around us were bad-tempered passengers, grumbling and sweating into their Life Shop T-shirts. If I looked down I saw identical grey sandals everywhere, starting to look scuffed and a bit worn around the straps.

By the time I struggled off the bus my head ached, my feet were killing me, and the thought of the walk home was too much. Charlie whinged as I put him in the wheelchair. Feeling that somebody was watching, I looked up.

Our car was parked opposite the bus stop. Mum was getting out, smiling, sensible and kind, like she used to be. She'd come to meet me.

13

'I was thinking you'd been a long time,' she said, but she wasn't cross. She was warm and kind, taking fretful Charlie out of my arms while I folded the chair and shoved it in the boot. 'I thought you'd be on that bus, and it's a long walk on a hot day, what with Charlie and all his trappings, and your shopping.' She stopped talking, and looked round. 'Where's your shopping? Have you been all that time and didn't buy yourself anything?'

I can't remember what I said, and I didn't care much. She looked so sorry for me that I wished I could have told her the truth – but I didn't see how I could.

'Never mind,' she said. 'I see Charlie's got a little flag. What did you do about lunch?'

I haven't a clue how I answered that, either. I can't tell you how much I was loving this. Mum hadn't been like this for months. The spell was broken. I was soaking up all that mothering warmth. I was a cat by the fire, the cat rolling in the catnip, the cat lapping the milk…

'… and it just occurred to me,' she said, 'that you'd be glad of a lift home from that bus. I don't know why I didn't think of it before. Honestly, my brain isn't my own these days.'

'I think it is,' I said, and couldn't keep the smug smile off my face. *Cat got the cream*. At home I snuggled Charlie down on the settee while Mum brought us cold drinks, and while she was out of the way I checked my mobile.

There wasn't a word from Kieron, and when I tried to phone him I couldn't get through. I tried to send a text, but it failed. I checked that the envelope was still in my bag. Just in case… The Life Shop might be losing its grip, but even now the directors could be at work in that sinister room in Pellmarket, getting themselves together again.

I only hoped that Mum – my new, interested, concerned mum – wouldn't ask too many questions about what we'd done and where we'd been. I didn't feel like telling a whole string of lies. It wouldn't be right, and besides, I was too tired to make anything up. But Charlie sorted that one for me. He woke up as Mum brought the drinks in. He wriggled himself to sitting up and drank with those two wide, picture-book eyes looking over his cup. He had that focused look, and I knew he was gathering himself up for something.

Go for it, Charlie, I thought. You can do it.

'Train,' he said.

Was that all? After what he'd been saying all day? Say it, I thought, but I didn't want to push him. He'd shut up and say nothing.

'There's a train on your flag,' said Mum.

'I train,' said Charlie. Getting better, but this called for some tactics on my part.

'No,' I said. 'Charlie doesn't know about trains, do you, Charlie? You don't know about trains.'

He killed me with a glare, and came out with it. *'I go on train!'*

Mum stared at him, then at me, then back at Charlie, and then she remembered to shut her mouth. I think Charlie was waiting for her to say something.

'Yes, I took him on a train,' I said, as if it was no big deal. 'Just to Pellmarket and back for a treat. I thought he'd like that.'

'More train?' said Charlie hopefully.

'Give me a chance,' I said, and Mum still couldn't say anything.

The phone rang early that evening and I jumped, but it was only Dad to talk to Mum. They were on for ages, and I was worried that Kieron might be trying to get through – but when they stopped talking he still didn't ring. Nothing on the mobile, either. I was thinking of going round to see Fern in case he phoned home, then it rang again, and I hit the ceiling.

It was Mr Harris, the piano teacher, and I smiled so my voice sounded polite. It was good news – he wanted me to play for a couple of church things, and the money was good – but I just wanted it to be Kieron.

'Mum,' I said, 'when I was out this afternoon, did anyone call me? I mean, late this afternoon?'

'No...' she said slowly, but she had that 'checkout closed' look that you get when you're trying to dredge something out of the memory. 'But there was something... oh, yes! Dr Montgomery phoned, to bring forward the date for Charlie's next appointment, but he particularly wants you to be there. I think it's because you've had so much to do with Charlie's music.'

'Cool,' I said, with my hand on the door handle.

'The only thing is,' she said, 'it's on your birthday. It's not exactly a birthday treat, is it?'

'It's cool,' I said again, and it was, but at that time I would have said an afternoon in a brick oven was cool, just to get away. 'We won't be at the hospital all day. There are loads of places we can go. We'll have fun.'

'If you're sure,' she said, but I was halfway down the path. I nearly ran all the way to Fern's house, where the door stood open and I could hear Fern laughing. In a second she was halfway down the stairs and leaning over the banister.

'What are you standing there for when the door's

open?' she said. 'D'you want a Coke?'

As we carried our drinks upstairs, I remembered Fern's room the way it had been all summer, looking like a Life Shop warehouse. Face it, I told myself. I walked in and gasped. I could only see rainbows. There were rainbows everywhere, pinned to the walls and littering the floor.

Yes, I did see some Life Shop stuff too, but only when I looked round to see where it had all gone. She'd shoved the lot into a corner, out of the way. The T-shirts were in a rumpled heap with the grey sandals on top of them, and the cleared floor was covered with bright rainbow drawings. I stepped carefully over them.

'What do you think?' she said. 'I was just going to phone you and ask you to come over and look at these.'

It was like looking at a vision. 'It's your restaurant,' I said.

'Course it is!' said Fern, and laughed. 'It's called…' she giggled nervously, '"Rainbows and Fountains". Or "Rainbow Sparkle".'

'Last time I saw you, you wanted to wear a cardboard box on your head and dish up beefburgers,' I said.

'Get a life!' said Fern. She looked at me as if I'd lost the plot, then laughed. 'Look, this is the real thing. We serve everything fresh, with loads of fish, rainbow trout a speciality, and it's built round a courtyard with fountains, and I have to find some way that the fountain catches the light and makes rainbows. I should ask Kieron how…'

I interrupted. 'Has he phoned? Today?'

'Him?' she said brightly. 'He never phones. Look, I want the crystal to make rainbows, too, and when people are sitting outside…'

'… they get fountain spray in their puddings,' I said, but it was so, so good to hear Fern gabbling and giggling like a waterfall, never mind a fountain. She was back, bubbling with life, laughing.

'You could sit on the edge to have your coffee,' she suggested, and I said you could drop your ciabatta in the water, and before we knew it we were making up daft things about ducks, fishing nets, performing seals, self-catching trout and waterproof spaghetti, and Fern laughed so much she spilt Coke on the grey sandals and the nearest T-shirt. I went downstairs to get a cloth.

'I've gone off those sandals,' she said. 'And the T-shirt. You can have them, if you like.'

'No thanks,' I said quickly. Mrs Miller came busying up the stairs to see what sort of a mess we'd made and stood in the doorway, getting her breath back.

'Lorna wanted to know if Kieron phoned, Mum,' said Fern.

'Well, no, he hasn't and I'm worried,' she said. 'With all that trouble they're having in Pellmarket and thereabouts, and our Kieron in the middle of it.'

Fern gave that sound that's half a giggle and half a raspberry, but I wasn't laughing. I tried to sound normal.

'What's happening in Pellmarket?' I said.

'Oh, haven't you heard the news, they've had power cuts all over the area, they've had power surges and computers crashing and phones cut off, and nobody can get a signal and nothing's working. The electricity don't know when they can get everything running again, I tried phoning our Kieron, but he's unobtainable, I've even tried phoning his work, but there's no answer from there, either, are you all right, Lorna, are you sure? You don't look well. And, I forgot to ask, how's little Charlie?'

I went home and found Mum watching the news. They had a report about power cuts causing chaos in Pellmarket, but nobody could explain what had caused them.

'It was OK when we left,' I said. What else could I say?

Of course, I still wondered what I – what *we* – had done. Fern, Mum and Mrs Miller were free now, I could see that. Something was right. But not everything, not until I knew Kieron was safe.

'By the way,' she said, 'when you were out, Charlie said something about "keen" or "keyring". Do you think it could have been "Kieron"? But why would he be talking about Kieron?'

'No idea,' I said. If Charlie was getting as bright as that, I'd have to take care what I said in front of him.

All that evening, there was no word from Kieron. When I

went to bed I slipped the envelope under my pillow, but I couldn't sleep. I tried not to think what might have happened to me if Charlie hadn't waded in with Peter Rabbit, but I couldn't help worrying about Kieron.

I tried to read and listen to music but I couldn't concentrate on anything, all that long, long night. I tried to sleep but I couldn't do that, either. I thought, I imagined, I hoped, I cried, I even prayed. I drifted off and dozed and woke again, and it was still dark. Morning was never coming, never, never.

Sooner or later, if I didn't hear anything, I'd have to do as he said and use the card. But how, exactly? Taking it to the police was all very well, but I don't think you can bring charges against anyone for trying to get a teenager to sign a contract. Besides, I knew that at least one top police officer was on the Life Shop's side. For all I knew, he still was. He might not be the only one.

If the Pulse had any strength left, it could be fighting back. If I wasn't happy about taking the card to the police, what about the media? Should I send it to somebody in television, or a newspaper? But the Life Shop had friends there, too. They might destroy it.

I knew there was a way of showing pictures on the computer, and Kieron had his own webpage. I hadn't a clue how to do it, but if I could use Kieron's computer, and if there were some instructions somewhere, perhaps I could post up the images on his page and show it to the world. I didn't know how to do it, but I'd work that out. If he hadn't phoned – say, by nine, no, by ten – and if I hadn't thought of anything else, I'd try it.

There was no point in trying to sleep. I got up and ran a bath with loads of bubbly stuff in it. Then, of course, after all that lying awake, the warm bath made me drowsy. By the time I got dressed I was a bit dizzy and out to lunch. Charlie was sitting on the landing in his pyjamas, with my mobile phone in his hand.

'Effone,' he said, and held it out to me. 'Effone ring.'

I'd snatched it from his hand before I remembered to say thank you very much, and what a clever boy, and hug him. There was a text waiting for me, and my fingers shook so much I could hardly press the right buttons. It could be anybody. It could be Fern, it could be one of those stupid messages trying to sell you something…

The text marched across the screen. It was the kind of message mobile phones are made for: *'CU SOON. I'M OK. RU? K.'*

It wasn't much. But it was everything.

14

I watched the news that lunchtime. The power was back on in Pellmarket, and they thought the chaos had been caused by a power surge from a rogue computer or something. Maybe I should have felt guilty, but when I looked at Charlie with banana round his mouth I just laughed, because Charlie and I had made all that happen. Oops. I was giggling out loud like an idiot who laughs at nothing, and Charlie laughed too, though he didn't know why. Then the next thing was Mum shrieking, 'Ouch!' and, 'B-b-bother it!' She came in limping, and sat down to clutch her foot.

'I just stepped on one of those stupid chime bars,' she snapped, flexing the hurt foot. 'I got them out last night in case Charlie wanted to play them, but he's lost all interest in them, and I never tidied them up.'

'I'll do it,' I said. I took my bowl of muesli and went

through to the kitchen where a wasp buzzed crossly against the window and the chime bars lay on the floor. They looked so tacky. I knelt and made myself touch them, because I mustn't end up getting phobic about the Life Shop. I'd just found a hairline crack running down the length of the first one when Mum and Charlie came in.

'The B's cracked,' I said. I checked out the rest, tapping them with the little beater, deliberately *not* playing that tune. 'B's cracked, A's flat, E's lost its paint and G's got a screw loose. If Charlie's lost interest in them, they may as well be binned.'

Charlie came to have his sticky face and hands wiped, and he didn't even notice the chime bars. There was a discordant clang as I threw them in the bin, then Mum swatted the wasp with the Life Shop's catalogue and binned that, too, and in the middle of all that the doorbell rang.

'Door,' said Charlie, and waddled off. OK, it isn't far for most people to the front door, but it was a long way for Charlie without his sticks. He did it, all by himself, but I had to help him with the handle.

And there was Kieron, so real and untidy and so much himself, with every mark and every detail about him right, and even a few – sorry – spots just where I'd remembered them. He had a smug, self-satisfied grin on his face – oh, just seeing him safe was all too much to hold, all that happiness had to find a way out, and it was OK to throw my arms round him and hold him tight, because he's only my best friend's brother, after all.

'Keyan,' said Charlie, and Mum said, yes, he had been saying, 'Kieron,' last night, then she said something to Kieron about 'Would you like a drink once Lorna puts you down and lets you breathe?'. She left us alone while we drank orange juice, and he told me what had happened.

'I went back to the Life Shop, like I said I would,' he told me. 'Nothing much happened. The fire brigade were there but there wasn't much for them to do apart from opening jammed doors. I was in time to see the directors being gently led away by the ambulance crews, but they were all walking. Nobody was hurt, they just looked dazed. But last night was a meltdown. No power, no phones working. I couldn't have got out if I'd wanted to, the trains were all over the place, if they were running at all.'

I held my drink in both hands. 'Excuse me,' I said. 'You mean you *didn't* want to get out?'

'Well, yes, I did, but I wanted more to stay around and see what would happen. Early this morning, the power was on again and I went to the Life Shop.'

I swallowed hard. 'Idiot!' I said.

He shrugged. 'I was still supposed to be working for them. Everything was locked up and a few dazed-looking people were standing around outside to tell us that the staff were to go home, the Life Shop was closed until further notice and we'd be paid until the end of the week. So I packed and got the next train home.'

'Fern's designing restaurants again,' I said.

He grinned. 'Yes, I found that out,' he said. 'She's OK. So's everybody, as far as I can tell.'

'I was scared,' I admitted. 'Really scared, when I thought about what we'd done. I thought something bad might escape from the Pulse, and sort of – I don't know – infect everyone, somehow.'

It sounded feeble, but Kieron didn't laugh. 'Yes, I wondered about that,' he said. He was watching Charlie scribble with some crayons, drawing something that might have been 'Lo', or a train, depending on which way up it was. 'But it's cool. Whatever was in the Pulse, it can't live out in the open. The life that it drained out of people is finding its way home.'

He swigged back his orange juice. Then he put down the glass and looked out of the window. 'I'll tell you what I think,' he said. 'All the Pulse could do was to take life – soul, personality, whatever – and transform it into its own energy. But it couldn't handle a Peter Rabbit! Something that simple started upsetting its mechanism, for a start.'

'It didn't think much of my arm, either,' I said.

Kieron suddenly sounded solemn and older. He still didn't look at me.

'I don't think it was just your arm,' he said. 'The Pulse knew about you, it was expecting you. It was ready for

130

you. But it didn't get what it wanted – your future. You did something really stupid – stupid as far as the Pulse was concerned. You put yourself in danger to rescue a toy for Charlie. You play the piano, but you risked losing your arm.'

'Well, you'd do anything for someone you love,' I said, but he went on.

'The Pulse couldn't make sense of you risking yourself like that,' he said, 'so it went into some kind of spasm. You wrecked it.'

'Charlie helped,' I said, and Charlie looked up with a grin full of mischief. 'Oh, and I've still got your digital card.'

'Keep it,' he said. 'In case we ever need it.'

'Kieron,' called Mum, coming into the room. 'You got out of Pellmarket just in time. There's just been something really strange about it on the radio. After all that trouble that night, they're finding the oddest things lying around on the streets this morning.'

'What odd things?' asked Kieron.

'Party things,' she said, with a puzzled little frown on her face. 'Streamers. Candles. Cake icing. Balloons. And gorilla suits, of all things.'

'*Gorilla suits?*' I repeated.

Kieron leaned back in his chair. 'The party-packs warehouse has blown,' he said. 'I told them not to put re-igniting candles in there. Sorry about that, Lorna, you won't be able to have a Life Shop de luxe birthday party now.'

So I hit him.

I want to tell you about my birthday because it was so cool, but I must tell you the rest about the Life Shop first. Only there isn't much to tell.

It just disappeared. There was a bit on the news now and again because it'd suddenly gone out of business and people were demanding their money back, and hundreds of people in Pellmarket were out of work. All those big names I'd seen in the Pulse Room denied knowing anything about the collapse of the Life Shop and said they were just shareholders, but they all lost face after that. They all had to resign from their posh posts, and the judge narrowly missed going to prison for fraud. Nothing much was heard about them after that, but I did hear that the former head of a satellite station ended up selling hot-dogs at a cinema and one of the generals admitted to an alcohol problem. Poor Trevor McLean had a minor breakdown and resigned his seat, and never took part in politics again. Cassandra Catto was found guilty of something – fraud, or fiddling the books, something like that – and had a short spell in prison. She never did much after that, though somebody told me she does cheapie adverts for a cable network.

Suddenly everyone was chucking out their Life Shop

catalogues and saying the clothes weren't that great, really, and there was nothing special about the kitchen stuff. The grass grew in the Millers' garden. The birds came back.

So it's over. I can't get over the feeling that something might still be around, but maybe that's just me being a wuss and worrying too much. I hope so. It's like the way soldiers who've been in a war sometimes have nightmares about it. Even if they've been on the winning side, they still have nightmares.

I've kept the digital card. You never know.

And now, I want to tell you what happened on my birthday.

15

We had to be up early, not just because you do, on a birthday, but because we had to get to Charlie's appointment. Fern was coming with us, to do some window-shopping while Mum and I took Charlie to see Dr Montgomery; then we were meeting up to go and eat somewhere. Mum bought me this really nice top that was just the kind of deep-red colour I love, and so glitzy that I wouldn't have dreamed of buying it for myself, but it looked great. She'd chosen exactly the right style, and the best thing was knowing that she'd thought about it, and looked for it, and cared about getting it right. She said she'd enjoyed going shopping for it, really shopping, going out and meeting people. And it was nothing to do with the Life Shop! Fern bought me a book that we'd read during the Tudor project, which she knew I liked, and Kieron gave me a poster with a polar bear on it. That was really sweet, because boys can be clueless about presents and I honestly, truly, straight up, hadn't expected anything from him. And Charlie gave me a big noisy kiss and a picture with 'Charlie' in big, colourful wonky letters and 'L' for Lorna, and loads of kisses. He must have worked really hard at it.

There was a card from my dad and a little cheap-and-cheerful bracelet, a sort of token present. That was disappointing, because Dad usually makes an effort for birthdays and Christmas to make up for not being around the rest of the time. But there was a little note in the card saying, 'Ask Mum about present.'

OK, he didn't have time to buy me a pressie so he'd slipped Mum a few quid and asked her to sort something out, but I wasn't going to let it spoil my day. Then Mum told me.

'Now, about your present from your father,' she said. 'Do you remember when you played at a wedding, early in the school holidays?'

Of course I did, and I said so.

'Well, one of your dad's friends was there, and he knew who you were, and he told Dad how well you played. Dad was very interested, he didn't know you were that good. He rang and asked me about your music, so next time you played in church he sat at the back to hear you.'

'*Dad* came to hear me?' I said.

'He did, and then he wanted to know who taught you.

He hadn't realized you weren't having lessons any more, so that came as a shock. So he sent me a cheque for your piano lessons for the next year, and if you want to do the exam, he'll pay the fee.'

For a minute I couldn't say anything, and when I did open my mouth, nothing came out. Then I said, 'Piano lessons?' It was like saying a charm.

'Of course, if that's not what you want...' began Mum.

'No!' I said. 'It's exactly what I want, I just...'

I just couldn't believe it. I couldn't take it in, and, yes, I felt so bad because I'd just been thinking Dad was a cheapskate who couldn't give an old teabag about me. Just having the lessons was going to be wonderful, but it was more than that. Dad cared about me. He'd come to hear me play. Good thing I hadn't known he was there, or I could never have concentrated.

Sometimes your birthday doesn't feel like your birthday, and you have to remind yourself about it. But that day was a real, authentic, hundred per cent birthday. My dad had done something about my music. And then...

We loaded Charlie, Charlie's stuff, and ourselves into the car and whizzed off to Newcastle with Fern and Charlie in the back going over all the singing games we'd practised. Fern had given me one of those cards that sings 'Happy Birthday' when you open it and she'd smuggled it into the car, so of course Charlie was having a great time, opening and shutting the thing all the way up the dual carriageway and braying with laughter. His volume control isn't too good in a closed space, and much as I love him I was glad he was next to Fern's ear and not mine. She just laughed and said he was practising it for Dr Montgomery. We dropped Fern off near the station and went on to the hospital.

'Come on, then, Charlie,' I said. 'Wow them.' We had the wheelchair with us but he walked from the car park, lurching like a sailor, but walking.

As usual they took him to a white room and weighed him, measured him, chatted to him, observed him walking with and without the sticks, and watched how he played with the toys. Dr Montgomery just smiled over the top of his glasses in his reassuring way. The staff were making notes, but I couldn't tell if they were impressed. (Charlie wasn't trying to impress, but I wanted them to know how much he'd achieved. I wanted to show him off.) He sat on the floor with the multicoloured building blocks and made a tower, but it wasn't just a straight column tower, it had shape. It was a castle, and what's more, it stayed up. When he ran out of bricks he looked for something else to put on the top and added a book of nursery rhymes, a small orange plastic saucepan, and a doll. That was quite a hefty doll, Barbie's bodyguard or something, and it did for the tower. It toppled over, and Charlie screwed up his face and whacked at what was left.

'Charlie!' said Mum. 'I'm sorry, Dr Montgomery, he gets

cross sometimes. I think it's my fault, I had to do a lot of extra work this summer. I don't think I had enough time for him.'

'Well, somebody did,' he said, and he gave me such a swift glance over his glasses that you wouldn't have noticed it. 'He's made extremely good progress.'

Charlie picked up Peter Rabbit. 'Music?' he said. 'Where panno?'

The staff all looked at each other and wrote it down.

'Sorry,' said Mum. 'He thinks everybody has a piano. He likes his music exercises. Oh, and Lorna took him on a train, he liked that.'

'I go on a train,' said Charlie with a grin, and they all wrote that down, too. I wanted to cheer.

'You really needn't worry about the odd flash of temper,' said Dr Montgomery kindly. 'It's because he's growing up. If he cares whether his tower falls down, it's a very good sign. A *very* good sign. And we're getting real sentences. Lorna, shall we take him to the music therapy room and see what he makes of that?'

Somebody else came to talk to Mum, and I went with Charlie and Dr Montgomery to the music room. At the piano we did 'The Teddy Bears' Picnic' and one or two easy-peasy exercises, then Charlie said, 'paxing', which I think meant 'practising', and climbed on Dr Montgomery's lap for a hug. By then he was getting tired – Charlie, not Dr Montgomery – and he went quiet and gazed into space.

I'd been wondering if Dr Montgomery would say anything about those Life Shop vitamin tablets, and whether I should mention it myself, but he raised it now. He was good like that.

'I'm very glad you sent me those pills,' he said. 'I followed it up at once. You weren't the only one, a number of my patients had been sent medication by the same people.'

'What was in them?' I asked.

'Oh, they wouldn't have done him any harm,' he said, 'but they wouldn't have done him any good, either. They were a mild tranquillizer, so they would have kept him quiet and calm, that's all. He'd never get excited about anything or be inspired by the things around him. He wouldn't have cared about going on the train, for a start. He'd be as good as gold and a doddle to look after, but only because of being doped. He wouldn't have made any progress. You've got a bright little spark here, and he may occasionally hit you with Peter Rabbit – of course, he has to learn not to do that – but he has a strong spirit.'

'Oh, he has that,' I agreed. Dr Montgomery didn't know how strong. Not even Charlie knew what he'd done. He'd taken on the Pulse and won, just by being Charlie. By knowing what he wanted. And being determined to get it. Without him I'd never have dared put my hand into the plinth. My superhero brother. But I couldn't go through all that with Dr Montgomery.

'I tried to phone the mail-order company,' he said, 'but

I could never get through to the right department. It now appears that the company is no longer trading, and a good thing, too. But I'll keep a weather eye open, in case it ever reinvents itself with another name.'

'Could it do that?' I asked, but Dr Montgomery was no longer listening. Charlie had picked up the word 'name', repeated it, and was reaching out to the desk for a pencil. Dr Montgomery handed one to him and he scrawled 'Charlie', the way he does. It was a thinner pencil than he's used to and it looked as if it was written upside down in a mirror in Russian, but Dr Montgomery was well impressed.

'Well, Charlie, what very good writing!' he said. 'Has Lorna been teaching you?'

''Orna birfday,' said Charlie, and I remembered that I'd meant to show Dr Montgomery the card he'd made me. I took it out of my bag and spread it out in front of him, and he studied it as if it were his granny's long-lost will.

'Lorna,' he said at last, 'someone – and I suspect it's you and your mother – has worked miracles with this little boy. You should be very proud. If he goes on like this, there's no knowing what he might do.'

The bright flash of hope in my heart must have shown on my face. His next words brought me down a bit.

'Of course, he's never going to win a Nobel prize,' he said, 'and don't believe anyone who tells you otherwise. But he has great potential, and he's working hard to fulfil it. Most of us only use a very small part of our potential. Charlie has to use all of his.'

'What about…' I said, then I wasn't sure how to go on. Charlie wriggled down and sat on the floor, all golden-haired and blue-eyed, and I couldn't imagine him ever being different – let alone not being there at all. But Dr Montgomery knew what I meant.

'He may live to be an adult,' he said simply, 'or he may not. We simply don't know. All you – all *we* – can do is to go on making each day as good as it possibly can be, and you're already doing that.' He bent over Charlie. 'Now, young man, what were you telling me about a birthday?'

Charlie did his party piece and sang something that was meant to be 'Happy Birthday' and sounded like a fire alarm, and before you could say 'musical cards' Dr Montgomery had arranged to meet us after he'd finished his clinic. He took us all out to this funny little restaurant that we would never have found on our own. It had wooden beams and flagstone floors and settles – those long seats with high backs – and quirky corners, because the walls looked as if they never fitted properly. There were pictures of elves peeping through windows and sitting on toadstools, and the milkshakes were to die for. Fern didn't even attempt to redesign it, she would have gladly taken it over just the way it was.

It was one of those shining days you remember forever. I wriggled back into the corner of the settle and thought of my piano lessons, and took it all in. Mum was soaking it up because she hardly ever gets to go to places like that, and have a treat. Charlie was eating very slowly because he was more interested in drawing on a paper napkin. (We'd left his crayons in the car, but Fern lent him a lippie and let him get on with it.) Dr Montgomery got everyone happy and talking, and I sent a text to Kieron to let him know what a great time we were having. Even when Charlie knocked Mum's drink over, the waitress was really nice about it and brought another one, so it didn't matter.

Settled back against the tapestry cushions I thought what a funny mix of people we were, and what an odd place it was, and how Charlie brought us together. We seemed to be against everything that the Life Shop ever stood for. There was nothing neat and tidy and packaged about us. We were part of a happy, messy, unpredictable world, where sometimes children are born disabled and dads run away, but there's always love in there somewhere, and friends turn up and meet in amazing restaurants, and drinks get spilled… and it's life, but you can't shop for it, you can't order it the way you want it and send it back if you don't like it. All you can do is run to meet it, and hold out your arms to it when it runs to meet you.

Charlie finished drawing. He climbed up to my lap and pushed the paper into my hand. Mum saw it properly before I did.

'Oh, my goodness!' she said, and pulled out a tissue.

'Let's see, Charlie,' I said, spreading it on the table. Then I saw what he'd written. And without help, all by himself, in chunky, shiny, lipstick letters like fat wet red kisses, he'd written:

All Lion Children's books are available from
your local bookshop, or can be ordered via our
website or from Marston Book Services. For a
free catalogue, showing the complete list of
titles available, please contact:

Customer Services
Marston Book Services
PO Box 269
Abingdon
Oxon
OX14 4YN

Tel: 01235 465500
Fax: 01235 465555

Our website can be found at:
www.lionhudson.com